HIS SECRET BABY

A Small Town Second Chance Romance
Accidental Love

Jessica F.

©Copyright 2023 by Jessica F.

All rights Reserved

ISBN: 978-1-958151-43-3

In no way is it legal to reproduce, duplicate, or transmit any part of this document in either electronic means or in printed format.

Recording of this publication is strictly prohibited, and any storage of this document is not allowed unless with written permission from the publisher.

All rights are reserved.

Respective authors own all copyrights not held by the publisher.

Table of Contents

Title Page..1

Blurb..7

Chapter One..8

Chapter Two..15

Chapter Three..22

Chapter Four..29

Chapter Five...35

Chapter Six...42

Chapter Seven..49

Chapter Eight...56

Chapter Nine..62

Chapter Ten..69

Chapter Eleven...76

Chapter Twelve..82

Chapter Thirteen..89

Chapter Fourteen...95

Chapter Fifteen..101

Chapter Sixteen...108

Chapter Seventeen..115

Chapter Eighteen 121

Chapter Nineteen 128

Chapter Twenty 135

Chapter Twenty-One 141

Chapter Twenty-Two 148

Chapter Twenty-Three 155

Epilogue 162

Other Books in This Series 170

Blurb

I promised the grumpy billionaire only one dance.
But I ended up giving him more than what I wanted.
I have no idea who this man thinks he is. Yelling at my friends like that...
Once I ran at him like a bull in beast mode, his looks did little to affect me.
Sure, he's hot, but also a jerk sometimes.
I don't even know why I danced with him and took him to my place.
I loved the night we spent together, kissing his handsome face and letting him touch me in all the right places.
I think I'm falling for him.
And the last thing on his mind is to start a family.
Now he's gone, and I'm expecting his baby.

Chapter One

Jag

"Population, two thousand one hundred ninety-two people." With wide eyes, I stared out the window of my RV as the driver pulled into the small town of Shiner, Texas. "Home of the brewery that I hope to take to the next level."

Miss Petty, my assistant and an old friend of my late mother's, chimed in, "If you manage to talk the owners into letting you invest, this will make your fiftieth investment. How proud your mother would've been, Jag. Only thirty-five, and you reached billionaire status at the tender age of thirty. If your mother could only see you now."

"Mom sees me, Miss Petty. I know she does." As for my father, I'd never known the man. Mom had been a super-independent woman, using a sperm donor and in vitro to produce me, her only child. I had expected my strong and independent mother to be with me forever. Only, cancer doesn't care what anyone expects. It took her away from me when I was twenty. And at that moment, I had made a promise to my dead mother that I would find a way to do the best I could from then on. And I'd done precisely that.

Investing came easy to me. Mom had a killer life insurance policy that left me with over a hundred thousand dollars. So, I did what came naturally to me and invested it in stocks, then bonds, and then I went for more. I just kept growing that money she'd left me, expanding my areas of investment. And, after a while, I found myself at the top of my game.

Now, I was taking it to small towns. Shiner, Texas, was the first in this new series of investments. They had a brewery that produced a Texas staple—a dark lager beer styled for the American palate but produced in the traditional German way. It was a success in Texas, but I'd also found there were exceptional sales in almost every state in the U.S.

I wanted more, though. I wanted to take this thing right back to where its roots had grown deep and gnarly. *Germany*.

A tough market, for sure, but I had my bets on the tasty brew making it big in the beer capital of the world. All I had to do was talk the owners into letting me spend some money trying to do that by becoming an investor.

They didn't have any investors thus far, and from what I'd heard, they had no interest in finding any. They didn't trade on the stock market either. So, I had my work cut out for me—but only if I decided the business was worth my time and money.

First, I wanted to see what kind of place this brewery was. Would it be able to handle all the extra orders that would come its way if I was successful at marketing in Germany?

I needed to know the quality of the staff. Would they work overtime if necessary? Would the management be up to snuff when the big orders came in? Would they hire more people if it meant production would have to go into twenty-four seven shifts?

I needed to know if the people behind the beer had it in them to step up, or this thing could never be taken to the next level. Not liking to fail—most successful people try to avoid that at all costs—I'd do my research before I would put my money on the line.

"Podunk," the driver, Tex, called out. "We have arrived, boss."

The old man I'd hired to drive my new, extremely tricked-out, forty-foot, Class A recreational vehicle was a necessity—the thing was a behemoth that I wasn't about to even try to drive on my own.

"Please, don't call every small town Podunk," Miss Petty chastised him.

"I don't mean no disrespect. It's just what I call these small, look-alike towns, Miss Petty." He drove down the main street. "All the buildings in these little towns look the same to me. Old, brick, and painted in different colors to help each little business try to stand out a bit."

The buildings, built in the early twentieth century, lined both sides of the main thoroughfare of Shiner.

I'd spent the first years of my life in a small town.

Wyoming, New York, looked like pictures on Christmas cards in the winter months. I still remembered the cold winters and the way they chilled me to the bone. When I was eleven, Mom moved us away from there—all the way across the country to California. The small town was left behind. Modesto became our home for the next nine years—until she was no longer with me, and I had to go it on my own.

Of course, Miss Petty was there with me through all the cancer treatments and then the funeral. She had worked with my mother at the courthouse. Both had been court reporters. Miss Petty only left her job when it became necessary for me to hire an assistant to take care of my expanding business. She insisted on helping me as much as she could.

"The RV park I've booked is near the high school. Take a right here, Tex," Miss Petty directed the driver.

"It says on the website that the majority of the citizens are of German or Czech heritage." Smiling, I recalled the lively dances the locals in my own small hometown of Wyoming had held on special occasions. "I wonder if there will be any polka dances going on while we're here."

Peering at me over her horn-rimmed glasses, Miss Petty said, "We're not going to be here for any longer than three days. Less, if you can make that happen. You do have the meeting in Fredericksburg on Monday. And after that, we have to get to New York for the christening of your friend's baby. A godfather is a big responsibility, you know."

Why my friend from high school had asked me to go to New York to become the godfather of his newborn son, I did not know. I figured he assumed I would shower the child with gifts his whole life. But I wasn't into babies—or kids, for that matter. I was into me and all things associated with me.

"I'm not about to take any responsibility for Jason's kid," I let her know. "I'll do the little ceremony thingy and be the kid's godfather. But honestly, that's all I'll do."

Her furrowed brow told me she didn't understand something about what I'd said. "Then why agree to do it at all, Jag?"

"I don't know why I agreed." He'd called, asked me if I'd be his kid's godfather, and I had just said yes without thinking about it at all. "Impulse, I guess. I mean, who wouldn't want to be called a godfather? Maybe that's why I said yes. Anyway, we'll go to New York, and I'll do the thing. So, keep me on track, Miss Petty. Do what you do best—keep things moving and me getting to the next place, like you've done for the last ten years."

"I will do as I have always done for you, Jag. I made a promise to your mother that I'll never break." Her smile told me she really cared about my success.

"Thanks, Miss Petty."

"Jag, I've told you a thousand times to call me Samantha."

"My mom would rip me a new one if I ever did that, Miss Petty. I was never allowed to call any grown-up by their first name. You know that."

"Jag, you are a grown-up now. I'm only fifteen years older than you. I think we can put those childish ideas of yours to rest."

"Nope. I can't do it, Miss Petty. It's ingrained in me now." Looking out the window, I saw something that interested me. "Look, a diner. I bet they've got killer chicken fried steak in there."

"I can't eat anything like that," Miss Petty said as she ran her hands over her slim hips. "I've got to watch everything that goes into my mouth. I wasn't blessed with a thin frame, so I must work to keep myself fit and trim."

I never could figure out why the woman felt that she had to look as close to perfect as she could get. She didn't even date anyone. But I never asked or commented. My mother had raised me better than that. "Well, I'm going to walk over there while you guys set up camp."

"You do that, Jag." She sat on the sofa, seatbelt buckled, eyes on the road in front of us. "I'll make sure Tex sets everything up."

I watched the old man's shoulders slump and knew he wasn't super keen on her making sure he did things to her expectations—which would mean everything had to be perfect.

Miss Petty made sure things were always perfect for me. She thought that was her main job. It made life easy for me, so I didn't ask her to do things any differently. "You do that. I'm gonna stroll down Main Street. I think it will give me a clearer picture of the way the people in this town think. Are they movers and shakers, ready to make some serious cash? Or are they lackluster and lazy and care nothing for money?"

Tex laughed. "You won't find many movers and shakers in small-town Texas or any small town anywhere for that matter. Folks from small towns are there for a reason. They don't care for the hustle and bustle of big cities. Money ain't the be-all and end-all for them."

"I came from a small town, and then I lived in a big one. I like the hustle and bustle as well as serenity at other times. You never know how people are until you find that out for yourself. You can't go around making assumptions that all people who live in small towns don't care about making money."

"I'll go with my gut on this," he said as he pulled into the RV park. "You want me to stop in front of the office, Samantha, so that you can go inside and see where they want us?"

"Yes, please, Tex." She looked at me, pulling off her glasses. "Want to come with me, Jag?"

"Why?" I asked with bewilderment.

"Never mind." With a sigh, she nodded. "Okay, I'll sign in by myself then." It was her job. "Okay."

She left the RV, and Tex turned his chair around to face me. "So, you gonna load up on some of that beer for us to sample this evening? I'll fire up the barbeque, and we can drink the night away."

Hanging out with a couple of old people sounded like a nightmare to me. But I could provide the beer for their evening without me in it. "I'll have some beer delivered in an ice chest for you guys. I'm going to hit the town to get a taste of it. But you two enjoy your time here in whichever way you want."

"Thanks, boss." He'd driven the better part of the day, bringing me here from my home in Dallas. I knew he was ready to relax.

I had homes in Los Angeles, New York, Dallas, and Miami. Well, I had given the Miami home to Miss Petty. But it had been one of my original homes.

I had to give her something so she could spend time away from work—she wouldn't take a vacation for anything. So, I gave her the gift of the Miami home and the cars that I'd bought while there. She'd taken a week off to spend it there when I first gave it to her. But she'd only gone back a handful of times since I'd given it to her, five years ago.

Miss Petty was devoted to her job. I guessed I was lucky that she was that way. I could've gone through many assistants, like most people I knew in my tax bracket. With her, I knew I wouldn't have to look for someone else to take her place for many years until she was ready to retire.

Miss Petty wore a frown when she came back into the RV. "What is it?" I asked.

Shaking her head, she looked at Tex. "It's the last space on the left." Her eyes turned to me. "If the staff here is anything like the rest of the town, you won't find the brewery worthy of your investment or time."

"And why do you say that?"

"Well, the lady at the desk couldn't bring herself to get up off her ample behind to do her job of taking the credit card and swiping it to get the payment for the lot rent. I had to walk over to her and hand it to her. And then she pointed out a rack of pamphlets, letting me know that if I wanted to do any sightseeing, I could pick as many of them as I wanted. I assured her that I had no interest in seeing the sights and that we were in town on business."

"What did she say to that?"

"She didn't say anything to that. She just pointed at a filthy fridge and told me that we could buy ice from the office before five, when she closes the office for the night. I told her that we have an icemaker in the RV and wouldn't be needing any."

"So, she's a little on the lazy side," I said. "That doesn't mean everyone in this town is. You can't judge an entire population by one person. I'm sure she's just bored with her job. Who wouldn't be? Sitting there, waiting for people to come in, and then having minimal time to say anything to them sounds insanely boring to me."

"Yes, I'm sure it's a dull job. But she could put some pep into it." Her jaw set, she mumbled, "I told you this was going to be a waste of time."

"Yes, I know you did." But she wasn't always right. "I came from a small town."

She jerked her head, looking at me with her mouth open as if she was shocked by what I'd said. "Jag! You come from Modesto, California. That is no small town."

"Originally, I came from Wyoming, New York, and that was a small town. And I want to give back to small-town America. I've made something out of myself, and I want to give back to the places and people who are the heart of our country."

"I'm just afraid that you're going to be disappointed in the people that you want to help. You're not like them, Jag. You're—well, you're better than them."

I wasn't sure how to respond to that. I knew that I was an exceptional man. I had a drive that not many people had. I knew my strengths and my weaknesses, which were few. But that didn't mean that I was better than anyone. Not really. It only meant that I'd found my way in life. I'd found what worked best for me. And if I could help anyone else find that, then I would.

"So, Tex is going to make a barbeque, Miss Petty. And I'm going to have some of that beer sent over here for you two. Enjoy the night. I'll be out and about."

"You don't want me to come with you?" she asked.

I wasn't about to take her with me. "I want to meet people on my own. If I have someone with me, it won't really work out. So, you guys enjoy your night, and I'll see you when I see you."

Now, to see what this little town has to offer.

Chapter Two

Millie

"How long do you think that thing is?" Rachel asked, as we all looked through the large window of the diner where we'd all worked for forever.

"I'm not that good a judge of things like that, but I think it's like twenty feet or so," Laurie said.

"It's longer than that," I said as I watched the huge RV cruise slowly down the main street. "And you know that thing must have cost the owner tons of money."

"It's brand new, I bet," Rachel said as she wiped a table down while looking out the window.

"It sure looks like it," Laurie said. She leaned on the handle of the broom she'd been using to clean up after the lunch rush. "Who do you think that is anyway? A country singing star?"

"They have their names on the things they ride in," I said. "And they ride in busses, not RVs. It has to be someone with money, though. But, other than someone in the music biz, who would come here?"

"We got beer and polka dancing, but not much else," Rachel mused. "Maybe it's a polka band coming to play at Benny's tonight."

"Not in that," I said. "It's got to be someone big. Way bigger than any polka band." I laughed as I thought about something. "We don't even know if that thing is gonna stop here. I doubt it will. Why would it? What does Shiner have to offer whoever is in that gorgeous mansion on wheels?"

Laurie laughed too. "Yeah, like whoever is in there is gonna come here. What would their reason be? Come to see if our chicken fried steak is better than the last tiny town's?"

"Well, it is better than anything else you can get around here. Yoakum ain't got shit on us where chicken fried steak is concerned," Rachel said with a smirk.

"It's a bigger town than ours, Rachel," I reminded her. "So, it does have shit on us."

"This town is famous," Laurie said. "Yoakum ain't famous."

They were getting way off topic, as usual. So, I brought the conversation back to where it had been before they threw it off track. "I haven't even ever been inside something that nice. Have any of y'all?"

"Hell, no," Laurie said. "Ain't none of us been inside anything that nice. Never will either. Things like that—well, we ain't supposed to know about any of it."

"Why not?" I asked. "Why not us?"

"Cause we're small-town people, Millie," Rachel stated. "People like us don't get to even see the inside of something like that."

"Hey, it's turning toward the high school," Laurie said.

The cook, Freddie, came out from the kitchen. "What are y'all gawking out the window at?" He wiped his hands on his greasy white apron as he came to find out what we were doing. "Ain't y'all got a mess to clean up after that lunch rush? You gals shouldn't have time to stare out the window." Suddenly, his eyes caught what had taken our attention. "Oh shit! Would you look at that? What a beauty she is."

"Why do men call all things mechanical she?" I asked. "I don't get it."

"Girls ain't meant to get it," he said with a grin, revealing his missing front tooth.

"You ever seen anything like that in Shiner before, Freddie?" Laurie asked, her eyes glued to the majestic thing.

"Hell, no. Shit like that doesn't come around these parts, girl. It looks like it's headed to the school, though. Maybe the governor is in there. Maybe he's gonna speak at the school."

"You're an idiot," Rachel said with a smirk. "If the governor was coming here, then there would be reporters everywhere. Haven't you ever watched the news? That's how things like that work. He doesn't miss a chance to get the media to record whatever he does. It's got to be someone else."

The RV did not stop. Instead, it drove past the school, giving us an excellent view of its back. Which was still pretty amazing. "It's leaving town." I looked away and walked toward the back, where I still had things to do. "We might as well get back to work."

"What would a life like that be like?" Laurie asked as she moved the broom to sweep up the crumbs left by our guests.

"Who the hell out of us would know, Laurie?" Freddie asked as he opened the door and stepped outside. "Hey, it's turning into the RV park over there. I can barely see it from here, but it sure looks like that to me."

Going back to the front, I walked outside with the rest of them, craning my neck and squinting my eyes to see if what Freddie had said was actually true. "No way. There's no way anyone who has a thing like that would stay here."

"Hey, what about the people who own the brewery?" Laurie asked. "Maybe it's them. They got loads of money."

"They also have a home here. So, it's not them," I pointed out. "But who the heck could it be?"

"They've stopped," Freddie said. "In front of the office. I bet they're just asking for directions, is all."

"You know that thing must have GPS," I said. "But there's no way they're gonna stay there. That place is a shithole."

"It's the best this town has to offer," Rachel said, moving up to her tiptoes. "I can barely see it. What's going on? Are they parking it or pulling back out of there? Like, what could they be doing over there?"

"It's still parked," I said. But I knew they wouldn't be staying. No one driving a thing that nice would have anything to do here."

"I still think it's a country singer. Maybe not someone from Nashville, but someone from here in Texas," Laurie said. "You know, one of Texas' own."

"We would know if anyone worth a hoot was playing at the bar tonight," Rachel said.

Freddie nodded in agreement. "Tonight, my cousin Louie is the DJ down there. Which reminds me that we all should go down there tonight."

"I'm off tomorrow," I said, looking at Rachel, who was also off the following day. "Wanna go together?"

"Who's gonna watch my kids, Millie?" She had two of them, and they were as rowdy as a box full of puppies.

"Maybe I can talk my little sister into watching them," I offered. "What you gonna pay?"

"All I've got is a twenty for that." Shaking her head, she said, "I doubt she'll do it for that. Momma's had them all day, so I know she won't watch them. And you know how we get, girl. We'll be out all night. There's no way your sister will take twenty to watch them all night long."

"Who knows?" I said. "She might. I'll ask her if you want."

"If she agrees, then sure," she said. "I'll be your date, Millie."

"I'll let you know later about what she says. I don't wanna go alone."

"I'll be there," Freddie said, then winked. "I'll be your date, Millie."

There was no way that was going to happen. "Um, thanks, Freddie, but I don't want anyone in this town to get the wrong idea. Rumors could spread like wildfire."

"That's okay with me," he said, then blew me a kiss.

And that's exactly why I can't go with you.

"Anyway," Rachel said to break the awkwardness. "If she says she'll do it, I'll come by and pick her up and take her to my place to watch them, then I'll bring her back home in the morning."

"I'll let her know and see if she'll do it." The RV began moving, and I found my mouth hanging open. "No way."

"Are they pulling in?" Laurie asked. "Are they gonna stay the night here in Shiner?"

"I think they must be staying," I whispered. "Who knows? They might even come over here to eat. They were sure going slow when they went past here."

"You girls better get this place spic-and-span then," Freddie said. "And the manager is gonna be here soon too. All this lollygagging around needs to stop."

"You too, Freddie," I said as I walked back inside, feeling butterflies moving around in my stomach with the excitement of what might happen if the people who were in that fancy RV did come to our diner. "That kitchen is a greasy mess. Get it cleaned up. I can smell the old grease you've been using. Go pour it out and put some new oil in the fryers. We need to make this place sparkle if they're gonna show up here. What if they're famous or something, and they talk about our place being a filthy dump?"

"We might all lose our jobs!" Laurie shouted as she got to work sweeping the floor. "I've got the floors."

"I've got the tables," Rachel said. "And I'll make sure the checkout counter is clean too."

"I'll tackle the bathrooms," I said. "Let's make this place shine. It ain't often that we have guests of their stature in here. It might even be some bloggers, for all we know. This could be something! This could land our little diner and the town of Shiner on the map if we all work hard to make their experience a great one."

"We are already on the map, Millie," Rachel said. "The brewery, remember?"

"Yeah." I did remember the brewery. But the town could use more. The lunch rush had consisted of two older couples who always ate lunch here on Tuesdays and Fridays. There had been quite a few workers from the brewery too. All locals. No out-of-towners come to see our famous brewery. Only the locals kept the diner open.

I'd worked at the diner since I was sixteen. It had been around for years before that too. We were a mainstay for the locals. But they gave lousy tips, and us waitresses only made a few dollars an hour. There was no way any of us girls were going to get rich or even close to being in the middle class with the job. But it was our home—our town. And we didn't want to leave it behind. So, we made it work.

"They probably won't come here," Laurie said as she looked at all of us. "But if they do, who will get to wait on them?"

Rachel and I exchanged glances as Laurie bit her lower lip. Whoever waited on their table was sure to get a good tip. Maybe even a great one.

"Hey," I said as an idea came to me. "How about we all help out with them? One of us can be the main waitress, but the other two can help in other ways too. I can help Freddie in the back to make sure the plates not only taste great but look great too."

Rachel looked at me with discriminating eyes. "Yeah, your hair is a mess right now. Plus, you've got a gravy stain on the front of your shirt."

I looked down and found a brown patch right in the middle of my white shirt. "Dang it! I didn't even see that there." Running my hands through my hair, I felt the tangles. "Out of you two, I'm going to have to say that Laurie looks the best. So, she should wait on them. Rachel, you can help out by making their drinks and getting their appetizers ready so that they won't have to wait long at all."

"They'll give me the tip," Laurie said. "And then I'll split it three ways, between all of us."

Through the kitchen window, Freddie shouted, "What about me? What do I get out of this?"

"You get paid more than we do, is what you get," I shouted right back at him. "We don't even get minimum wage."

"Oh, yeah. I forgot about that. I'll shut up."

"So, let's get busy," I said, then went to clean the restrooms.

We all busted ass for the next half hour. Luckily, no other customers came in while we were working so hard. Just as I came out of the women's bathroom, cleaners in both hands and sweat dripping off my forehead, I saw a tall figure walking down the sidewalk. "Someone's coming!"

Freddie looked out of the kitchen window. "I saw someone walking out of the entrance to the RV park. I didn't say anything because I didn't want you girls to freak out."

"Damn it, Freddie!" Rachel shouted as she pulled the rubber band from her disarrayed ponytail and redid it. "You should've warned us."

Laurie looked into the mirror behind the counter, fixing her hair and practicing her best smile. "Welcome to the Shiner Diner, y'all."

"It's just the one guy," Freddie called out from the kitchen.

"Oh, okay then," Laurie said. "Welcome to the Shiner Diner, you."

"Just say the first part and leave the other out," Rachel said.

I ran around the corner to the kitchen, the door swinging shut behind me. Just then, the bell rang as the door opened. The silence stunned me as Laurie didn't say a thing, and neither did Rachel.

What the fuck, guys?

"You work here?" the deep voice of a man asked.

I ran my hand over my face with agitation spreading through me. "She's gonna mess this whole thing up," I whispered.

"Um, huh?" Laurie asked.

"You have on a uniform of sorts," the man said. "So, do you work here?"

"Um, sure," she said.

The sound of something crashing to the floor made me flinch as Rachel screamed, "God damn it!"

"You okay back there?" the man asked.

"Um, yes," Rachel said. "Laurie, seat him."

"Oh, yeah," she said as if she'd forgotten what her job was. "You want to, you know, sit?"

Holy shit! What's going on out there?

"I was going to want to sit down and eat, but I'm not sure now. This place is clean and all, but you got a shit show going on here. Is the cook as dingy as you girls are?"

Laurie didn't say a thing. Neither did Rachel. I couldn't believe what was happening. But then Laurie finally spoke, "You from that fancy RV we saw come into town?"

"Do you always ask your customers personal questions?" he asked. "What's wrong with you? Who the hell is in charge here? Anyone at all? Look, I wanted to try your chicken fried steak, but you and your little dish-breaking cohort back there don't seem to be very good at anything so far. Think you can pull yourselves out of whatever stupor you two are in so that I can have some fucking food? Or do I need to go elsewhere?"

There's no need to be rude!

Chapter Three

Jag

On the verge of getting things under control in the crappy little diner, I saw the kitchen doors swing open. "What now?"

A black hairnet covered a riotous mane of what seemed to be dark-blonde hair on a young woman with flared nostrils and red cheeks. Brown eyes glared at me, and I was fairly sure she was about to start bellowing like a bull for some reason.

Good God, is the entire town mentally unstable?

"Look here, mister," she said between gritted teeth. "You don't have to talk to them that way. Who do you think you are? Coming in here, not knowing a dang soul, and mouthing off like that?"

"Excuse me, madam." I tried not to laugh at the little lady with a big attitude. "This place is a wreck. And those two are more than clueless."

"Stop it!" She stomped her little black slip-proof shoe. One finger moved into the air as she readied herself to light into me. "They are not acting like themselves at all, and I will have you know that normally, they are very professional."

"I highly doubt that." There was nothing professional about any of this. "Where is your boss? Do you even have one? I would think that if you did, they would've come out here by now to fire you all."

Looking over her shoulder at the other two waitresses that stared at her with slack jaws and wide eyes, she huffed, pulled her shoulders back and squared them, then looked back at me. "It's pretty obvious that your looks have turned them into jelly. I'm sure you're used to that, though. Most guys who look like you would be more on the charming side rather than acting the arrogant way you are behaving. Would it hurt you to be nice?"

"If my looks are what has affected them, then why aren't they affecting you in a similar manner?" It would've been nice if the girl would've been just as speechless as the other two.

"Pretty boys ain't my thing, mister."

"So, you like ugly guys?" I had to laugh. "I mean, the hairnet isn't super attractive, but you're not exactly hard on the eyes. You can do better than some old ugly guy."

"Some people are ugly on the inside. You get what I'm saying?" Crossing her arms over her chest, she glared at me. "You gonna order something or just try to boss everyone around?"

This chick is unbelievable.

"If you haven't noticed, I haven't even been seated yet. I really can't imagine how this place has stayed in business if this is the way you treat paying customers." I pivoted on one foot, turning to leave. There was no way I would spend one cent in the place with the rude behavior I was dealing with. "You can thank yourself for losing my business." I turned back, smirking at the waitress with the attitude of a pitbull. "Just so you know, I always tip a minimum of twenty-five percent—even if the service is lousy. When I get good service, I tip up to seventy-five percent."

"Sure you do," she said with her own smirk. "I bet you stiff the waitresses more than you don't."

"You don't even know me."

"Sure I do. Rich jerk who thinks he's better than everyone else. Loves demanding things. Loves ridiculing others. I know you." One of her hips cocked to one side, and she placed her hand on it. "Go on, leave if you want to. But you'll be missing out on the best chicken fried steak on Earth if you do."

"I highly doubt that." The girl had the oddest game I'd ever seen. If she thought she was going to get me to stay, much less eat anything these fools had a hand in, she was certifiably insane.

A lanky brunette came out from behind the wall where I'd heard the crash of glass earlier. "She's right," she said. "We were sort of stunned by you when you came in. Has anyone ever told you that you look like a young Elvis Presley? It's sort of breathtaking."

"Come on, Rachel," the mean waitress who enjoyed berating me said. "He's no Elvis. Sure, he's got dark wavy hair and blue eyes, but that's about it."

The blonde who had been the one who was supposed to be my waitress shook her head. "Nope. He's the spitting image of the man. The young Elvis—not the old, fat Elvis. And what about all those muscles he's got going on? He's the total package, Millie. You've got to admit it."

"I won't admit a thing, Laurie." The little meanie I now knew was named Millie eyed me, scanning my body as she judged me with her eyes. "Just because you're attractive doesn't give you the right to come in here and act like a jerk."

"Just because you're attractive doesn't mean you can talk to me this way," I shot right back at her. "I'm sure you're used to all the guys around here dropping to their knees for you, but I'm not like them. So you can take all your insults and shove them where the sun don't shine, little lady."

I watched as her hands balled into fists, her arms stiff as a board at her sides. "You can shove..."

"Millie," some man called out from the back. "Can I talk to you for a minute?"

"Go—talk," I said. "I'm out of here."

As I walked toward the door, the blonde moved to get in between me and the exit. "Wait. Please. She's just acting a little crazy. Millie's not really this way." She looked at the young woman who was stomping away from me to go and talk to whoever it was that had called her to the back. "Like—she's never been this way. This is my fault."

The brunette came to stand beside her, both of them now blocking my way out. "It's my fault too. Please, stay. Please, try the chicken fried steak. It's on the house. After all we've put you through, it's on us."

"Can I even trust the food here?" I wasn't so sure that I could. "I mean, look who just went into the kitchen. How can I be sure she won't poison me?"

"Millie's harmless," the brunette said with a smile. "I know she didn't seem harmless, but she really is. She'll calm down, and I'm sure she'll come and apologize to you."

It wasn't like I needed her apology. "To be honest, I'm not even hungry anymore." Gesturing for them to move, I asked, "Can I just get the hell out of here already?"

Dropping their heads, they moved away from each other so that I could leave. The blonde said quietly, "We really are sorry. Please, come back if you get hungry. You can eat here for free the whole time you are in Shiner. We're very sorry for what's happened."

The kitchen door swung open, and out came the little hell-raiser with an entirely different look on her face—a face that was really pretty when she wasn't glaring or smirking at me. "I am sorry." She held her arm out to the blonde waitress. "Laurie will be your waitress, and I will leave all of you alone." She looked at the other two. "I'll be in back if you need me for anything. I'll stay out of the way. I'm sorry I cost you two so much. I won't do that again." Turning, she walked away from us.

Watching her walk away, shoulders slumping and head hung low, I knew she really was sorry for the way she'd treated me. "Hey, Millie, right?"

She stopped and slowly turned to look at me. Calm speculation filled her doe-like brown eyes. "Yes."

"I'm Jag Briggs. And I'd like to apologize too. I didn't have to react the way I did." I knew I owed it to them all to say sorry for the way I'd acted and the things I'd said. Turning to talk to the others, I said, "You girls too. I'm sorry."

The blonde nodded. "Guess we all should be sorry for the way we acted, Jag. What a cool name. Your mom must be pretty badass to have named you something like that."

"She was," I said.

"Was?" Millie asked from behind me.

Turning back to her, I nodded. "Yeah. Was."

Empathetic eyes met mine. "Mine too."

So, she was without a mother too. "Your father still around?"

Shaking her head, she said. "No. They went together in a car wreck. Yours?"

"Never knew the man," I said with a shrug. "Lost Mom to cancer when I was twenty—fifteen years ago."

"That's rough," she said. "I was nineteen when we lost them, six years ago."

"Rough indeed. It's a sad thing to have in common with someone." My heart went out to her since I knew exactly how it felt to lose a parent. And she'd lost both of hers. "Anyway, sorry we all got off on the wrong foot. I didn't mean for anything like that to happen. I'm actually in town to find out some things about the brewery. Making enemies right off the bat seems like a pretty bad idea to me."

"Might be," Millie said with a smile. "We're cool now. I hope we are anyway."

"Yeah. We're cool now," I agreed.

"Care to sit by the window, Jag?" my waitress asked as she picked up a menu. The other girl walked back to where she'd come from. "What can I get you to drink, Jag?"

"What do most people from around here drink?" I asked.

"Sweet tea," she said.

"I'll try some of that then." I'd thought she would say the beer they brewed in the town. Seemed like I had been wrong. Looking at the blonde, I said, "Yeah, a seat by the window sounds good."

"Right this way," she said as she led me to a table for two. "Here's the menu."

"I know I want the chicken fried steak. But what about the side dishes?"

"Mashed potatoes, gravy, and green beans are what I always recommend. But the sides are all right there on the bottom left of the menu if you'd like to try anything else."

"No, that sounds good to me." I handed her the menu. "Is there a store nearby where I can buy some of the beer that's made here?"

"Two blocks down and one street back to the left," she said.

The brunette came back with the drink. "You don't have to go down there. I'll set you up. How much did you want?"

"A twelve pack." I'd promised Tex an ice chest of the stuff. "Don't suppose you guys have an ice chest that I can borrow."

"We sure do. We sell them. I'll pack one up for you and ice the beer down too. Is it going to your RV?" she asked, seeming like she wanted to help me out as much as she could.

"It is going there." Now that things had settled down, I actually liked the girls.

"I'll take it over there if you'd like."

"I did promise my driver and assistant that I'd have some delivered. Tex is the driver. He's making barbeque. Miss Petty is my assistant. She'll be there too."

"A barbeque, you say?" she asked with a cocked brow. "I'll pack up some potato salad, pinto beans, and rolls for them too. Do you think they'd like a coconut cream pie, or would they rather have a pecan pie? Never mind, I'll take one of each over there."

"That would be nice. I'm sure they'll sample both pies." I took a drink of the sweet tea and found it to be delicious. "Oh man, this is great."

"I'll take a gallon jug of sweet tea over there too. They might like something besides just beer to drink."

"They'll love it." I was glad I hadn't left the diner the way I'd planned to. "Thanks for doing all that, um, they called you Rachel, right?"

"Yes, I'm Rachel, and your waitress is Laurie." She hurried off to get the things to take to the RV, and I was left smiling away at her now-efficient attitude.

Laurie came out of the kitchen, carrying a tray. "I wasn't sure if you wanted soup or salad while you waited for your meal, so I brought both."

"You didn't have to do that." They were going way overboard for me now. "The salad is fine."

"The soup is the cook's specialty. Chicken enchilada soup." She put the small bowl down on the table then placed the bowl of salad beside it. "What kind of dressing should I bring you for the salad?"

"Do you have balsamic vinegar with olive oil?"

"No, we don't have anything like that. We've got ranch, thousand-island, blue cheese, and French dressing."

"Ranch," I said with what must've sounded like disappointment.

"I can run down to the store to see if they've got some of that dressing you asked for."

"No. Don't do that. Ranch is just fine. You girls have already done a lot for me already. Everything is cool now. No need to go to so much trouble."

"It's no trouble at all," she said, determined to make sure I was one happy customer.

"Laurie, they don't have that type of dressing at most stores. It's something the cook puts together. So, don't go to the store. Just bring me the ranch dressing, please."

"If you're sure," she said, one hand on her hip and the opposite eyebrow cocked.

"I'm positive." Digging into the soup, I loved the flavor. "And please, give my compliments to the chef. This soup is excellent."

"Glad you like it." She darted off to the kitchen to deliver my compliment and to get the salad dressing.

Moments later, she delivered the salad dressing, and I gave the plastic bottle a generous squeeze before stabbing the pile of fresh greens with my fork. "Yum." For a dinky diner, the meal—so far—proved to be above my expectations. "Is this Ranch dressing made in house?"

"Sure is," she said with a smile.

The cook had the main dish ready before I even had time to finish off the soup and salad, so I pushed them to the side and dug into the hot food. "You guys are quick."

"We try to be." She left me to enjoy the meal.

Halfway through the delectable chicken fried steak meal, I got a call from Miss Petty. "Did you get the stuff I sent over?"

"We did. It's all very good too. I tried to tip the girl who brought it, but she said everything was on the house. Tex and I are wondering how you accomplished that."

"I acted like a jerk is how I accomplished that." I cut another bite from the breaded steak, determined to finish every last bit of it.

"I don't see how acting like a jerk got you so much free stuff," she said. "Care to explain a bit further?"

"We all sort of acted jerky. Now, they're treating me like royalty." I looked around to be sure no one would overhear me before I said, "I'm going to pay far more than what all this is worth anyway. I'm not letting them give me anything for free. But they don't know that yet."

"That would be nice of you since you admitted to being a jerk in the first place. So, have you found something to do this evening, or will you be coming back here to join us?"

"I'm going to see if the little beer joint that I saw on the way over has anything going on tonight since it's Friday. If nothing's going on, then I might come back to the RV. But I am stuffed, so don't save anything for me. I couldn't eat another bite if I had to do it to save my life."

"If the bar does open, should I join you?"

No way in hell.

Chapter Four

Millie

Freezing to death as I took inventory inside the walk-in freezer, I jotted down the amounts of everything on a small notepad. The groceries had to be ordered before five, or they wouldn't be here on Monday, and then we'd have real problems. Not that the manager cared a lick.

Rory had been hired by his uncle, who owned the diner. As far as he was concerned, he was Shiner royalty and acted as such. He'd been due in at noon, but it was nearly three and he'd yet to show up.

Emerging from the cold, I shivered, closing the heavy door behind me. "Brrrr."

"I've got a coat hanging on the hook over there, Millie," Freddie said. "You should really wear one whenever you've got to be in there for any length of time."

"I was hot anyway." The whole crazy argument with the RV guy had riled me up. Thanks to Freddie calling me back, reminding me that I needed my job, I had been able to calm down enough to apologize. And things de-escalated after that.

"While you were in there, Rory came in," he let me know.

"Great." I headed to the office, which was way in the back of the diner. "Finally."

Rory, the manager, didn't seem to be there to work—he was looking at his phone while swiveling back and forth in his chair behind the desk. "You got the inventory done, Millie?"

Doing that was part of his job. At least, the last manager had done the inventory. But Rory didn't believe a manager was supposed to actually work. He thought delegating the work was what he was supposed to do. The only thing was that I was the only one to whom he ever delegated any work. "I've got it done."

"Great. Call and make the order then. Did you make next week's schedule like I asked you to?"

He'd asked me to do that every week since he'd come to work at the diner a year ago. "I do have it done. It's hanging in the kitchen."

Lifting his eyes off the phone screen, he asked, "Can I see it?"

"I've already taken a picture of it and sent it to your email." Picking up the phone, I got ready to call in the order.

"Send it to my phone too," he said. "Now."

"Right now?" I was about to make the order.

"Yes. Right now." He looked up from his phone again. "Please."

"Well, since you asked me so nicely, how can I say no?" With much exasperation, I stopped what I had been doing to send him the picture of the schedule I'd made, then got back to the ordering.

I heard his phone ding with the message I'd sent. "Got it. Can you see if the cook has any sausage? I'm dying for sausage with peppers."

There were all sorts of things on the menu for him to pick from, but he'd never picked anything off of it yet. "I'll put in this order, then go and tell him to make you what you want."

"But I need to know if he's got any sausage or not."

"He does. I just did inventory, remember? I know what he does and does not have."

"Well, get him to start making it now before you make the order. I'm starving. I haven't eaten a thing all day."

"You know that this order has to be in before five, right?" I had a bright idea. "You know, if you want me to do other things, you can call in the order. It's really straightforward, not hard at all."

Putting his phone face down on the desk, he looked at me with a furrowed brow. "I know it's easy. That's why I let you do it. Giving the cook my order won't take you but a minute, Millie. You've got a pretty bad attitude today. Better fix that ASAP, or you can go home."

I should go home. But then who would do all your work for you, jerk-off?

Shaking my head, I went to give Freddie the order. I had to admit that I might've had a bad attitude. I had been flustered most of the day. And I'd gone off on a customer, which wasn't like me.

I needed a break, is what I needed. I'd worked seven days straight without a day off. Two of the waitresses had come down with the flu, and that meant the rest of us had to cover their shifts. I wasn't the only one who'd worked straight through the week.

"Freddie, the master wants sausage and peppers. Think you can drum him some up?"

"Why can't he order off the menu?" he asked as he went to get the stuff he would need to make the meal our manager had requested. "And how does he know what kind of food we have to work with when he doesn't do any of the ordering?"

"Hell if I know. All I know is that I really need tomorrow off because I am burning out right now."

"Hey, come to the bar tonight. Tequila shots will be on me," he offered.

"I might just take you up on that, Freddie. Thanks. I need a mood-buster." Five o'clock couldn't come fast enough for me. "And thanks for talking me down when I got so angry earlier. I don't know what came over me."

"Yeah, me neither. But you put the dude in his place. The girls have been a little over the top with him, though. You'd better check with Rachel. She's got the tab for all the stuff they've given him."

I rubbed my temples—I hadn't meant for them to give him more than a meal. "Damn. I'll have to accept the responsibility for that since I was the one who said everything was on the house for him. Rory is going to chew me out."

"Maybe don't tell him," he said.

"That's stealing." I wasn't a thief. "I'll deal with the consequences."

"I just wouldn't tell him about it. But that's just me." He began cutting up the sausage. "It's not like he actually ever does any of the reports. He has you doing them all."

He wasn't wrong. I did do all the reports. I kept the books balanced. I did the man's job in all ways. But he did look over the things I did. "Even if he didn't catch me, I would know that what I did was wrong. It's a write-off anyway. And it was my attitude that caused the whole scene after all."

"You take on too much responsibility, Millie. You don't have to do that. Laurie and Rachel had a huge part in that. I don't know why they had to go all dumbstruck over that guy."

"Well, he is gorgeous. If he hadn't made me so angry before I saw him, I might've acted the same way they did. But fire was already blinding me when I went out there. I can see why they acted that way, though. It was my reaction that was over-the-top."

"It was a bit aggressive," he agreed.

"I just need to unwind. Take it easy for a bit. You know?"

"I agree with you." Tossing the cubed sausage into a hot pan, he began to work on cutting up the peppers into thin slices. "Tonight, you can dance away all your cares and start over fresh come Monday."

"That's right. I've got Saturday and Sunday off this week. I forgot about that. Since Carrina isn't sick anymore, she took over Sunday for me." There was light at the end of the tunnel now. "Thanks for reminding me, Freddie."

"We're all in this together, Millie. Don't forget that." Freddie was a nice guy and a pretty good cook too.

"Thanks, Freddie. It's nice to have you guys." Life hadn't been easy on me since Mom and Dad died. Six years on my own, making sure my younger sister had most of what she needed was no walk in the park.

It wasn't like our parents had left us much. The house had been rented, so we had to move out of the home where we'd grown up only a couple of weeks after they died. We couldn't pay the rent, and I wasn't about to ask for any favors from anyone.

I'd been saving some money and had enough to get us into a small apartment. We made it. We'd squeaked by. And that's how we lived—squeaking by.

I wasn't going to let my sister go the same route I had. She was going to college no matter what I would have to do. The plan was for her to get a degree, a good-paying job, and then take care of herself. After that, it would be my turn to try and make something more out of myself than just a waitress.

"Millie?" Freddie asked.

Shaking my head, I pulled myself out of my headspace. "Yeah?"

"You okay?"

"Sure."

"You just sort of zoned out and went into another world. But you didn't look happy in that world either."

"Oh?" I had no idea it had been that obvious. "Just thinking about things. I've got to get back to what I was doing. I'll be back in fifteen minutes to get my plate."

"It'll be ready and waiting for you."

Heading back to the office, I tried not to think about any of my personal problems as I picked up the landline to make the order. "It'll be ready in fifteen minutes," I let Rory know.

"Can you grab me a cold beer before you make that order, Millie?"

Staring at him in disbelief, I nodded. "As soon as I get done with this, I will do that for you. But I've got to get this order in. Otherwise, we're going to have big problems come Monday."

"Fine." He got up. "I'll go and get it myself then if it's too much trouble for you."

Go for it, jerk-off.

His attitude told me that I'd been doing way too much for the man. He expected me to do his job while waiting on him hand and foot. It was time I pulled back on some of the extra things that I did that were definitely not part of my job.

It wasn't like he was going to fire me for simply refusing to bring him food and drinks. I did all the real work he asked of me. And if he did fire me, then who would take my place?

Not everyone was eager to do his job for him. I only did it because I needed this job. Not that everyone else didn't need their jobs, but I really needed mine. There was no one else bringing money into our house. And I wasn't going to let my sister take a job when she had school to focus on.

A babysitting gig now and then was okay, but a job that she had to go to almost every day wasn't going to happen. Not as long as there was breath in my lungs. Myra needed to focus on school, not work.

After putting in the order, I heard the sound of the bell ringing as the door opened three times. The others needed me to do some actual waitress work with this many people coming in to eat. So, I went back out to the customers outside. The first thing I noticed was Jag still sitting at his table.

He wiggled his finger at me, gesturing me to walk up to his table. At first, I just stood there, looking at him. He really was quite spectacular. And he knew it too. A cocky grin on his chiseled lips told me he knew that I'd come to him with just the wiggle of his finger.

He's a cocky son of a bitch.

Now that there were other customers in the diner, I wasn't going to lose my cool the way I had before. So, I put on my professional face and went to him. "Yes, sir. What can I do for you?"

"I hear there's going to be a DJ playing music tonight at the bar down the street."

"Okay." I wasn't sure why he thought that he needed to tell me that.

Holding out a piece of napkin, he said. "Take this."

"What is that?"

"My number."

I shook my head—I wasn't about to call the guy. "I don't think–"

He took my hand and forced the thing into my palm. "Take it. Call me when you head over there. Rachel said you two are going to be there tonight. I'm picking up the tab for you two tonight."

"Oh, I get it. You want me to call you when it's time to pay. No thanks. I mean, that's nice of you and all, but you don't have to do that. We're not rich, but we're not broke either." That wasn't entirely true. I had a whopping ten bucks to spend at the bar that night. But I didn't want the guy to buy our drinks. Only I had no idea what Rachel wanted. "But I'll hold on to your number in case Rachel wants you to pay for her drinks."

"You're not getting it, Millie. I want you to call me when you go to the bar. I want to spend some time with you. Get to know you. Not Rachel. If I wanted her to have my number, I would've given it to her. I want you to have it."

"How long are you going to be in town?"

"Not long. Maybe a day, maybe two."

It was clear what he wanted from me. "Look, the stuff you got here is on the house. But I'm not part of that deal." Spinning around, I tried not to blow up at the man.

"Millie, wait," he called out as I walked away.

Lifting up my hand, I stuck my middle finger straight up so he would know for sure that he'd pissed me off and offended me entirely.

So the rich guy wants to have a one-night stand with the broke waitress he'll never have to see again. No thank you!

Chapter Five

Jag

What is with the attitude?

I hadn't meant to offend Millie with anything I'd said. But it was obvious that I had.

The manager of the diner had finally arrived. Laurie had told me who he was when he'd walked through the door. I wasn't going to tattle on the girls, but I had to talk to him before I left. I wasn't going to leave the place without paying my bill.

Laurie was busy with a table near me, so I waited until she was done then asked, "Can you send the manager over here?"

Her expression went to something akin to a deer caught in the headlights. "Why? Didn't we make things right with you, Jag?"

"Yes. Of course, you all did."

"I saw Millie flip you off. Is that what you want to talk to him about?" She sighed as she looked over her shoulder as Millie retreated, then she looked back at me. "She's not acting like herself. We've been overworked this last week. Can you please not tell on her? Rory already makes her do more than he asks from any of the rest of us. Please, don't make things harder on her."

"I'm not going to tell on anyone. I just want to talk to him. So, please send him over."

Looking nervous, she nodded. "Okay then."

I watched her as she went to him, they talked, and then he looked at me, nodding. But he didn't come to me. He went into the back, and then I saw Millie coming to me instead of him. "I didn't ask to talk to you," I informed her.

"I know. What is it that you wanted to talk to the manager about?" she asked, not looking at me at all.

"Why did he send you instead of coming to talk to me himself?" I found that rude and unprofessional.

"That's the kind of manager he is. He delegates. Anyway, what can I help you with?"

"Well, I want to pay my bill. So give it to me."

"No." She turned to walk away.

But I wasn't going to just let her do that. "Hey. Look at me, please."

With an audible huff, she turned and faced me. "I said it was all on the house, didn't I?"

"Millie, that bill is probably close to a hundred dollars. I'm not leaving you girls with that. I know you're going to get into trouble if it's not paid."

"It can be written off," she said. "You're free to leave."

"I'm free to leave?" I had to laugh. "And if I sit here and have a few beers, racking up that bill even higher, then what will you do? Will you give me the bill so that I can pay it?"

"Nope." She looked at the door as more people came in. "So, you want me to bring you a beer then?"

"No. I'm too full to even drink anything. I'm going to take a long walk when I leave here. I wanted to do some dancing tonight too. You know, to help burn off some of the calories I've consumed here today. That's why I gave you my number. Laurie said you're a killer dancer. I thought you and I might kick up some sawdust on that dancefloor tonight."

Her eyes leveled on mine. "And that's all you want from me?"

"Did you think I wanted more than to dance and buy you a few drinks while we get to know each other?"

"Why wouldn't I think that you wanted more than that?" she asked with narrowed eyes. "Don't think that I'm dumb just because I'm a waitress from a small town."

"I don't think you're dumb at all. From what I've heard, your boss relies on you heavily. He wouldn't rely on you if you weren't smart."

"So, you need me to help you with some aerobic exercise. And that's all. Right?"

"That and your engaging company. I've never met anyone like you, Millie. And now that I know you've been overworked this past week, well, I know that you need a night out and to have some fun."

Her eyes cut to the side, taking in Laurie. "Laurie has a big mouth."

"She was just looking out for you, is all. When I told her that I wanted to speak to the manager, she was afraid I was going to rat on you all. And you especially. You know—for giving me the bird. So, she told me how you all have been overworked and how the manager makes you do more than he asks anyone else. Which is wrong, by the way."

"I'm aware of that. But I need my job. I do what I have to do to make myself indispensable."

"The thing about that is that we are all fully dispensable. If you walked away from this place right now, he'd have you replaced within the week. So, maybe don't do more than what you're paid for. If you want to do extra work, make sure you're getting paid to do it."

"Easier said than done. But I don't expect you to understand."

"Why, because you think I've got loads of money?"

"I know you've got loads of money. That RV alone is worth more than I can even imagine. It's so expensive that I don't even have the slightest clue what it cost you. Not that I'm asking, because that would be rude."

"At least you recognize that it would be rude," I laughed, trying to lighten the mood. "You're right, though. I'm well-off. But I've earned that money. My mother raised me in the middle class. She was a court reporter, and that was the only income she had."

"Well, good for you."

"I'm trying to tell you that I didn't come from money. I know about having hard times."

Her brows raised only slightly. "You do? You?" Her head shook. "No. Not the kind of hard times I'm talking about. Times when the electricity got shut off and stayed off for the better part of a month until you'd made enough money to get it turned back on. Hard times like that."

"If you're struggling that hard, you might think about changing jobs, Millie. And I'm not saying that to be funny. I mean that."

"In case you haven't noticed, this town ain't got much to offer in the way of good-paying jobs."

"About that. Are the jobs at the brewery good-paying jobs?" I had to know if investing in the place was a good idea or not.

"Yeah, they make good money. But you need to possess certain skills to work there. Skills that I don't have."

"They don't have a training program to teach people the skills they need to work there?" I asked.

"I have no idea, really. I've never thought about working there. I came to work here, at the diner, when I turned sixteen and haven't looked anywhere else ever since."

Living in a small town didn't mean one should get pigeonholed into a dead-end job. "You and I should really hang out together while I'm here. I can help you in ways you can't even imagine."

"I bet." With a sigh, she shook her head. "I've got a lot to do before I get off in an hour."

"I hope I see you at the bar tonight." I knew I couldn't sit and wait for her to call me, or I'd end up sitting in the RV with Miss Petty and Tex all night long. And that sounded depressing. "Can you promise me just one dance?"

Her brown eyes softened as she looked at me. "One dance."

"I'll take it."

"You don't give up, do you?"

"Never. I wouldn't be where I am today if I had given up. But seriously, can you take me to wherever your manager is hiding out? I really want to talk to him."

"No, Jag. Please. Just let me handle things."

None of the girls wanted me to talk to their manager, so I decided not to force the issue. "Okay then."

"Thank you." She smiled, and it was like a ray of pure sunshine. "See you later."

"You sure will."

"I've gotta get back to work."

"See you later, Millie."

Still wearing that smile, she walked away from me, disappearing into the back and making my heart ache in the best way. "She's something else."

I knew that none of them were going to take my money. And talking to the manager was out. But I had to do something.

Looking at the man at the next table, I saw he had a pen in the pocket of his shirt. "Do you think I can borrow your pen for a second?"

"Who? Me?" he asked, looking a little confused.

"Yes, you. I'll give it right back."

Pulling it out, he leaned over and handed it to me. "Okay then."

I took one of the napkins left on my table and jotted down a note. Then I placed five one-hundred-dollar bills into the napkin. Holding the folded napkin in one hand, I handed the pen back to the man who'd lent it to me. "There you go. Thanks."

"You're welcome."

Getting up, I walked up to Laurie. "I'm out. You girls have a good night." I slipped the napkin full of money into the pocket of her apron without her noticing a thing, then left.

I headed back to the RV. I'd eaten so much that I wanted to change into workout clothes and do something to counteract all those calories. When I walked up to the area we'd parked in, I could smell the smoke from the pit still burning. Miss Petty and Tex sat on lawn chairs, beers in their hands, country music playing softly in the background.

"You're here," Miss Petty said. "I thought you were going to check out the town and didn't know when you would be back."

Patting my stomach, I said, "I ate too much at the diner. I'm going to change clothes, then take a run and work out a bit."

"So, no going out tonight?" she asked.

"Oh, I'm going out. After the run, I'll come back and get cleaned up, then head over to the bar. I've got a girl who owes me a dance."

Pulling the beer bottle from her lips, she asked, "You do? Already?"

"Yep." Striding into the RV, I changed and then went back out, finding the two of them talking quietly. But they both fell quiet when they saw me.

Miss Petty smiled. "I would join you, but I've already had three beers, so running is out for me."

"I figured as much." Stretching a little, I jogged in place.

"But taking a run in the morning would be nice," she said. "Would you mind running with me then?"

She didn't like to run alone, thinking it was unsafe. "If I'm not hungover, then yes, I'll take a run with you in the morning."

"What are the chances that you won't be hungover?" she asked with a smile.

"Fifty percent." I wasn't some lush who made a habit of getting plastered. But I had no idea what the night would bring. "We shall see how this little town rubs off on me."

"So, is this girl from the diner?" Tex asked.

"She's a waitress there. She's pretty. And seems smart too. But she's got herself in a bad spot and is being taken advantage of. I hope to be able to talk to her a lot while I'm in town."

Miss Petty looked confused. "Why would you do that?"

"She lost her parents when she was nineteen. I know the effects that can have on a person. If Mom hadn't left me the money I used to make investments, then who knows what would've happened to me. She's had it hard since her parents died. That was six years ago, and she's still right where they left her, working at the same diner, making the same kind of money. And she doesn't seem to know that she doesn't have to live a stagnant life."

Sitting up in the chair, Miss Petty's expression took on one of protection. I'd seen it often enough to know what mode she'd gone into. Protection mode. "Now, don't go letting this girl's sob story make you do something you shouldn't do."

"Like what?" I asked, purely out of curiosity. I would do whatever I wanted to do for Millie, or for anybody for that matter.

"Like give her some exorbitant amount of money to help her get out of this small town. She might be making up the whole story for all you know. You can't trust people you don't know, Jag."

"She's from here. She told me about her parents right in front of her coworkers. It's not a lie. And she's not some sob storyteller either. She's proud. She's not looking for anyone to hand her anything. Hell, she wouldn't even let me pay the bill I racked up at the diner."

"I thought you said that you were going to pay it anyway," Miss Petty said as she sat back in the chair.

"I did pay it. And then some. But Millie doesn't know that. Or at least, she didn't know it at the time I left. If she had, chances are that she would've chased me down to try to make me take it all back. Not that I would've."

"Just don't forget that we'll be out of here by Sunday."

"Yes, I know. I won't fall off track, Miss Petty. It's just a night out, and then we'll go from there." Running in place, I felt the heavy meal in my stomach and knew I had to get moving. "See you guys later."

"Hey," Miss Petty called out. "Maybe I should get dressed and go to that bar too. You know, make sure you're not getting taken advantage of."

"No, thank you." I took off, not wanting to talk about it any longer.

Miss Petty was always looking out for me. But the thing was that I wasn't the same naïve kid I'd been when she'd first come to work for me. I could take care of myself, and I had never been taken advantage of yet.

Plus, with her around, I wouldn't be on my full game where romance was concerned. And I wanted to be on my game with Millie. She wasn't like any woman I'd ever met. And I thought she should know that too.

If she'll just give me some of her attention and time.

Chapter Six

Millie

Kicking my shoes off at the door, I entered our apartment, dropped my ass onto the couch, and closed my eyes. "A whole weekend off. Is this a dream or what?"

"Um, talking to yourself, Millie?" my sister asked.

Opening one eye, I found her standing over me, arms crossed over her chest, eyebrows arched. "Sure."

"Sure?" She shook her head, moving her waist-long blonde hair, which was hanging in waterfall curls that draped over each shoulder. "What's this I heard you say about having the whole weekend off? You don't get weekends off."

"I know." The smile that formed on my lips wouldn't go away. "I had Saturday off, and one of the waitresses who's been out with the flu volunteered to take my Sunday shift. It's a miracle."

"I'll say." Falling onto the couch next to me, she lay on her back, propped her feet up on my lap, then asked, "When can I go and apply to work at the diner? I've been sixteen for five weeks now. I can legally work, you know."

"I want you to focus on school. But if you want some spending money, Rachel will pay you twenty for watching her kids overnight at her place tonight."

"You know, I've heard that other people make a whole lot more when they babysit."

"Yes, that's true. But they don't babysit for broke waitresses. You do. And that will earn you a place in heaven, Myra."

"Sure it will." Wiggling her toes, she urged me to massage her feet.

"Are you serious?" I pushed her feet off my lap. "If anyone is getting a foot massage around here, it's me. I've been on my feet more this last week than ever before."

"You don't like the way I massage them," she said.

"You're too rough." I was pretty sure she massaged them that way on purpose so that I wouldn't ask her to do it.

"Your feet don't exactly smell like roses after a day at work, Millie."

"Some little sisters would make a footbath of hot, soapy water to wash their big sister's feet before they rub them."

"You got to be kidding me." Laughing, she got up and walked the three whole steps it took to get to the kitchen. "Supper tonight is grape jelly on toast. Hungry?"

"Not even a little. At least, not for that. Do we have peanut butter?"

"A little."

"So, why not peanut butter and jelly sandwiches?"

"The bread is too stale for that. So, it's toast and jelly."

"That's not even healthy."

"Like anything we can afford is healthy, Millie." She put a slice of bread into the toaster before getting the jelly out of the fridge.

My cell rang, and I had to move so that I could pull it out of my back pocket. "It's Laurie." Swiping the screen, I answered her call, "What?"

"You won't believe this, Millie!"

"Believe what?"

"He left me five hundred dollars!"

There was only one person who would've done that. "That jerk!"

"He's not a jerk," she screeched at me. "He's an angel, is what he is. Rachel and I combined his bills, and they totaled seventy-three bucks. So we cashed out his bill so that Rory never has to know that we were going to give it all to him for free. I've divided the change of a little over four hundred into three parts. I gave Rachel hers and yours because she said she'll bring it to you when she comes to pick up your sister to take her to watch the kids. She also said to tell you to tell your sister that she's going to pay fifty instead of just twenty for watching her kids."

I didn't want to take Jag's money. "That man just won't listen." I was worried about what Rory would think of someone leaving us tips like that. "Did you tell Rory about the tips?"

"Of course not," she huffed. "Rachel and I are not stupid. He has no idea about this tip at all."

We were supposed to report all our tips. But we mostly never did that. "Let's just keep this a secret between the three of us then. Does Freddie know?"

"No. Rachel said it was best to keep it between us."

"Good." I had to admit that even though I was aggravated that Jag hadn't done as I'd asked him to, having the extra money did pep me up. "I'll call Rachel once I have Myra's answer. Thanks for calling to let me know, Laurie. Are you going to head over to the bar when you get out of work tonight?"

"Hell yeah, I am!"

"See you there then. Bye."

Myra looked at me, taking a nibble of the toast with jelly. "What was that about?"

"This difficult customer left Rachel, Laurie, and me a big tip that we split."

"How big?"

I wasn't about to tell her how much, or she'd try to make use of the extra cash. "It's going to all go on the electric bill anyway. And that reminds me, stop leaving the bathroom light on all night long. It's running up the bill."

"I hate waking up to pitch-black, Millie. It's one little light. How much can it be costing to leave it on at night?"

"Well, our bill is over a hundred bucks, so you tell me."

Biting her lower lip, she took a deep breath. "What about a small nightlight?"

"Sure. You can buy one with the fifty Rachel will give you if you watch her kids tonight."

"You said twenty."

"Yeah, it was twenty until we all got the big tips. So, you'll have fifty. You can buy a small nightlight. A really little one. And since you're in the kitchen, turn the fridge to a warmer setting. That thing is old as dirt. I'm sure it costs a lot to run."

"Maybe tell the landlord that we need a new one then." She reached in and turned the knob. "The things in here are barely even cool."

"It's not like there's much in there to spoil anyway." Getting off the couch, I asked, "So, can I call Rachel to tell her that you'll do it?"

"Hell yes, I'll do it. I'm not turning down fifty bucks." Laughing, she said, "See if she can buy frozen pizzas, and I'll make them for the kids."

"Will do." I called Rachel to deliver the good news.

"Hey," she answered my call. "What did she say?"

"She said yes. And she said that if you get frozen pizzas, she'll cook them so that you won't have to feed them tonight."

"Of course! That's a deal. I'll be over there in like an hour so that she can deal with them while I get ready. They found some candy in my mom's purse while she was watching them earlier and are acting like crackheads over here."

"I'll let her know. See ya."

Going to my bedroom, I began looking through the closet, trying to figure out what I should wear. "Myra," I called out for her.

She came to the room, leaning her shoulder against the door frame. "Yeah?"

"She's going to come for you pretty soon so that you can watch the kids while she gets ready. But can you help me pick out something to wear tonight?"

Moving into the room, she used her elbow to bump me out of the way. "You don't really have much in the way of clothes, Millie. And the only place to shop around here is the dollar store. So, that's out."

"Like I've got money to spend on shopping anyway."

"Oh, wait!" She turned around and took off out the door.

I had no idea where she'd gone off to, so I stood in front of my closet, searching for something decent to wear. Suddenly, she was back in my room, holding out a short black skirt, a red crop top, and a pair of black cowboy boots. "Where did you get those things?"

"Jasmine," she said. "She's the same size as you. Her mom bought her these when she was in the beauty pageant last year. She got like five good outfits from that thing."

"Jasmine is the best. Tell her thank you and that I will give them back to her clean and pressed." My little sister's best friend had come through big time. "Plus, she can have my free employee meal at the diner any time she wants."

"She's totally going to take you up on that," Myra said. "Go shower and wash your hair. Let it dry naturally too, so that it curls up. The natural look is in now."

"I'll see." I was sort of stuck on using the straightener to tame my unruly curls.

"Come on, Millie. Just do it. You've worn your hair the same way forever. Time to loosen up. Have fun. Be free for once in your life."

Looking at my little sister, I knew she was right. I needed to have a little fun and loosen up—at least, for one night. The responsible part of me could reemerge later.

"You know what? I'm going to do it, Myra. I'm going to be carefree tonight."

"Yes!" Jumping up and down, she laughed. "You should see the smile you're wearing right now, Millie. It's been ages since I've seen it. But there it is."

Taking over as the provider and something close to a parent at the same time hadn't been easy. But there was no one else to do it, so I'd had to. "I feel it too, Myra. It's weird, but in a great way."

After taking a long shower, I got out to find that Myra had already been picked up. Turning on some music on my phone, I connected it via Bluetooth to the speaker in my bedroom. Country music filled the air as I dressed, did my makeup and hair, then went out to the hallway to see myself in the full-length mirror.

Running my hand over my hip, I admired the way the black skirt fit me. It was short and sassy. The red crop top had the kind of sleeves that you could leave up or pull down to expose your shoulders. Pulling down one side, I moved my shoulder around, then pulled the other side down too. "Okay, strapless bra it is then because this is too sexy not to completely rock out."

After a quick change of bra, I put the boots on, then returned to the mirror to get a look at the whole package. My hair hung in tight curls to the middle of my back. I hadn't worn it this way in many years. But I had to admit that I liked the way I looked.

Myra had some cheap jewelry in her room, so I went to find a bracelet and maybe a necklace and some earrings to add to my outfit. I found some silver things and put them on, then went to look at myself in the mirror again. "Yes. This will work."

When my cell rang, I saw it was Rachel and answered the call. "You ready to go?"

"I'm outside. Are you ready?"

"I am. Don't freak out when you see me." Grabbing my purse, I headed for the door to meet her outside.

"Why would you say that? What did you do?"

With my head down, I walked down the stairs and all the way to her car without her recognizing me. "Just a little something different."

"So, are you coming or what?"

I opened the passenger door of her car. "I'm right here."

"What the hell?" She looked at me with astonishment. "Millie? Is that you?"

"It is me." I slid into the seat. "You look great."

"Um, thanks. You look—well, great too—but you don't look like *you*."

Laughing, I admitted that I felt like another person. "I'm going to be free tonight. I need some fun and relaxation in my life. I've got to say that not having to worry about where the money will come from to pay the electric bill is intoxicating."

"That's what you're going to do with the money from the tip Jag left?"

"I know it sounds boring, but you have no idea how great it makes me feel to know that I won't be sweating that damn bill this month."

"Your part is in the glovebox."

Opening it, I took the money out. A one-hundred-dollar bill, a twenty, and several ones. I couldn't stop smiling. "There'll even be money left over after I pay the bill. Looks like I can do a little grocery shopping too."

"You know, I haven't asked you this before, but now that you're bringing up how little you and your sister have, why don't you see about getting on government help? You know, you can get money for food and sometimes utilities and stuff. Your parents did die. You and Myra can get help."

"No." I didn't like taking charity. "There are so many others who really need it. People who can't work. I can work. Myra is going to go to college, and she'll get a good-paying job. We can manage with what we have. Things will get better—someday."

"There's no shame in accepting help, Millie."

"I agree. And if it comes down to it, I'll ask for help. But, for now, I've got this." In my mind, I had to keep striving and working to show my younger sister that working for a living was a thing we both could do. We didn't need anyone to help us out. We could do it all on our own.

"What about Myra, though?" Rachel asked. "She might like to have more than what you girls have now. It can't be easy doing this all on your own."

"It won't be this hard for much longer. She's going to graduate next year, and then she'll go off to college. I expect that she'll get a four-year degree. After that, she'll find a good-paying job. And then it will be my turn to go to school. You know, once she can pay her own way."

"You do realize that you're talking about like five, maybe six years from now, right?" she asked with a frown. "That's a long time."

"It's already been six years. You're right—it is a long time. But I've done it this long, and I can do it that much longer. My turn is coming. I just have to be patient."

"So, you think that waiting something like twelve years before you can do you is fair in any way?"

With a laugh, I let her know what I thought about that. "Rachel, I've found out that life is not fair. I can't expect it to be that way. At least, not for me. All I can do is give my little sister the chance my parents would've given me if they hadn't been killed in that car wreck. I can do that. I can wait."

"You're going to be over thirty before you get to do what you want. And if you want to go to college, that will add more years to the time until you get to do you, Millie."

"I can wait." I had the patience that it would take to do what was best for my sister before I did what was best for me.

I can do whatever I have to for my little sister. Whatever it takes.

Chapter Seven

Jag

"Cowboy boots, Jag?" Miss Petty asked as I walked out of my bedroom.

"Is there anywhere better to wear these things?" I asked her. "I mean, it's small-town Texas and there's going to be dancing. I can hear the country music playing already as it wafts through the air of the otherwise dead town."

"Honestly, Jag, how's this little bar going to stack up against the music venues you've been to in Los Angeles and New York? I wouldn't even bother going if I were you."

It occurred to me that Miss Petty might have become snotty since she'd entered my employment. "You do realize that this series of investments will be made in small towns all over the United States, right?"

"I do realize that," she said, then pulled a glass of red wine to her lips, stained with the same color. "That does not mean that you should go slumming through them all, Jag. It's beneath you."

"Slumming?" I didn't like that word at all. "I'm going now. Maybe slow down on the booze. It's loosened your mouth in a bad way, Miss Petty."

When I walked out of the RV, I found Tex still sitting in the same chair, looking up at the night sky. "Would you listen to that music, Jag?"

"I heard it while I was getting ready. Texas country music is something, isn't it?"

"It sure is. Nothing quite like it. You go on and have yourself a good time. Podunk towns like this one offer the most fun a young person can have. Enjoy yourself tonight."

"Have you been to many small-town bars in your life, Tex?" The thought had occurred to me as I was getting dressed that an outsider might not be welcome in the midst of the locals.

"I've been to quite a few of them, yep."

"Do you think I'll be welcome?"

"Mind your manners. Don't act like you've got anything more than anyone else. Don't be loud or crude. Most of all, be respectful of the women."

"I'm never crude. And I don't disrespect women. I think I'll be fine."

"If trouble breaks out, make a run for it. I'll make sure the RV stays unlocked in case you need to get in quick. You never really know how the locals will act once inebriated."

"So, stay sober and pay attention to my surroundings." I understood things now. "Thanks, Tex."

Walking out of the RV park, the smell of moist earth filled my nostrils. It was a clean smell that one couldn't find in a big city with so many paved surfaces. Around here, there was plenty of earth—dirt that many plants lived in. The abundance of trees, grass, and flowers gave the place a scent that I hadn't captured during the daylight hours. But night brought them all to life.

With the rest of the town quiet at nearly ten at night, most lights were out, save the streetlights that lined the main street. The bar was nestled near the middle of the buildings. Bricks that had been painted bright red glowed in the light. A golden glow showed me where the open door was.

The music that had drifted through the town became louder the closer I got. Laughter, hoots and hollers, people talking, glasses clanking—the sounds of the lively bar put a smile on my face.

Inside, I hoped to find Millie. Perhaps she'd be dancing with some cowboy she knew. Maybe she'd be playing a drinking game with her friends. Maybe playing a game of pool with some handsome man that might bring some jealousy out in me.

I wasn't sure what I'd find or what my reaction would be. And it was invigorating. Not knowing what was about to happen had never had me feeling so alive.

"How about I play some Koe Wetzel for you drunk motherfuckers?" the DJ shouted.

The crowd cheered, apparently super jazzed about the singer whose song the DJ was about to play. I hadn't heard of the person before, so I had no idea what was about to happen.

Tall, dark bottles of beer with yellow labels peppered the scene as the people raised them high, preparing for the song they all seemed eager to hear.

I stood there, mesmerized by the scene. This was it. This was small-town Texas at its very best. The locals all gathered at the watering hole, listening to the songs they all had grown to love, drinking the beer that many of them had helped produce.

This was it. This was real life in the town of Shiner, Texas. A Friday night. Some kid playing music from his homemade DJ booth that sat upon a stage meant for live bands.

Everyone had worked at their jobs during the day. The week was at an end and now the time had come for relaxing and celebrating life in their little part of the world.

They began swaying to the music as soon as it began. My eyes ran down the line of people who stood at the front of the stage. None of them were Millie. I looked at the people dancing behind the line of swaying people near the stage. None of them were Millie.

Scanning the small bar, I began to think she hadn't come out after all. Or she'd come and left even before I arrived. Or she just might not have come out yet.

I hadn't even asked for her phone number. That had been a mistake. For all I knew, she'd tossed the napkin with my number only moments after I'd given it to her. I knew I couldn't count on her to call me.

"Holy shit, I love this song," I heard a woman shouting.

My eyes went to her, finding her dancing with another woman. Head down, beer bottle held high, the woman moved slowly from left to right. Short black skirt, red shirt that showed off her creamy shoulders, and a pair of red cowboy boots that she never let leave the floor as she scooted her feet.

Throwing her head back, thick, dark-blonde curls cascaded over her bare shoulders, then down her back. Something hanging around her neck sparkled in the lights above her. "You sing it, Koe!"

"Millie?" I couldn't believe it. It sounded like Millie. But that hair, that killer body? Had all that been hiding behind the dull waitress uniform and hairnet?

Her head moved, swiveling around, and then her brown eyes met mine. A smile flowed over her lips, and she held her arms open, looking at me as if telling me to walk into those arms.

Moving through the people between us, I smiled right back at her. Her eyes never left mine as I came right up to her. Sliding her arms around my neck, she still held the bottle of beer. "Here's the dance I promised you."

Slipping my arms around her waist, I asked, "Is this the only one I get?"

Looking up at me, she shook her head. "You can have as many as you want. I'm in a very good mood tonight."

"As many as I want?" I liked the sound of that. "I'll take them all then."

"Then all of them you will get." She lay her head on my shoulder as we swayed to the slow-paced song.

Leaning my chin on top of her head, I inhaled her scent. Slightly flowery with a tropical side to it, the smell of her curly hair did things to my head that were similar to being on the verge of getting drunk.

"You dance well, Jag," she said, pulling her head off my shoulder.

"You do too." I couldn't believe her curls. "I've got to say that I adore your hair. Is this its natural state?"

"This is the real me." She downed the remainder of the beer then held it out. That was when I noticed the other waitress, Rachel, taking it from her.

"I'll go grab us more beer," Rachel said. "Looking good, Jag. Cowboy looks good on you."

"Thanks. And take this to the bartender." I pulled out a credit card. "Tonight is on me, remember? Tell them that I want to run a tab." I expected some argument out of Millie, but all she did was smile and lay her head back down on my shoulder.

"Got it," Rachel said, then danced away from us.

Holding Millie felt natural. Our bodies, flush against each other, fit perfectly. She was just the right height for me. Her arms lay loosely around my neck. My hands, clasped around her waist, found themselves a nice place to rest in the small of her back.

She didn't seem drunk at all, but she was most definitely much more relaxed than she'd been at the diner. "I like this version of you, Millie."

"I like this version of me too. Wish it was able to come out more often." Pulling her head up, she looked at me. "I like this version of you as well. Blue jeans and boots suit you, Jag."

"Funny, I didn't think you liked me much at all."

Her chest heaved as she sighed. "I was tired. I'm not tired anymore."

"Did you get in a nap?"

"No."

"What helped you get rid of that tired feeling you'd had before?"

"You did that. The thought of seeing you made me wake up. The thought of you holding me as we danced perked me right up. And the crazy thing is that I was right about how this would feel."

"How does it feel, Millie?"

"Like we've done this thousands of times before." She laughed. "I know that sounds crazy."

"Not at all. Holding you like this feels very natural to me. Do you believe in fate?"

"Not really. If I did, then I would have to believe that my parents were supposed to die that day. And I don't want to believe in things like that."

"What about the idea that you and I were supposed to meet?"

"You didn't come here for me, Jag."

"No, I didn't come here for you."

"And you're leaving. You're a big-city guy with big money and big dreams that you can actually make come true for yourself. I'm just a small-town girl with small dreams that I will struggle for years to make come even close to becoming true. If they ever do come true."

"Tell me about these dreams of yours, Millie." I wanted to know all about her. And I couldn't really remember wanting to know that much about someone I'd only known an extremely short amount of time.

"They haven't fully formed yet. But I know that I have to go to college to make them happen. Whatever the dream becomes, I need more to help me get there."

"So, a vague dream of someday being successful," I said. "Right?"

"Of course I want to be successful someday. But, I don't really know what I want to be successful at. I don't expect you to understand."

"But I do understand. When I first set out on this journey that I'm on, I didn't know what I wanted to become either. I began investing the money my mother left me through her life insurance policy. I wasn't sure where I was going to go from there. I didn't go to college. I was twenty when she died, but she'd been sick for years. When I graduated from high school, I did nothing—other than spend all the time with her that I possibly could."

"You knew that you were going to lose her, didn't you?"

"I did know that. The doctors kept trying to give us hope that she would make a full recovery. At first, I believed them. I wanted to believe them. But after the first surgery and the rounds of chemo, I could clearly see all that she'd gone through and the toll it had taken on her body. I knew that if the cancer came back, it would take her life."

"How long was it until it came back?" she asked with sad eyes that told me she understood me better than most people could.

"Six months. Three weeks after her last chemo treatment, she felt a lump under her arm. They'd taken both breasts, but the cancer still found some tissue it could invade and thrive in."

"I can't imagine how afraid she must've been."

Blinking back tears, I couldn't believe what she'd said. "You know, no one has ever said that to me before. Whenever I tell someone about my mom and what she went through, they only say things about how hard it must've been on *me*. But I thought just like you. I found it impossible to even start to understand how afraid she must have been. And I knew she was afraid. Even though she never let on that she was anything but optimistic, I saw it in her eyes from time to time."

"She wasn't afraid for herself," she said. "She was afraid of leaving you behind."

"You're right. At the very end, she told me that she was at peace with what would become of her. It was me that she worried about. It was me who would be alone in the world without her. And she apologized for not thinking things through when she planned her pregnancy."

"Babies sometimes just happen," Millie said.

"Most do. But I was planned. I'm the product of in vitro using an anonymous sperm donor. So, I am my mother's child, and that's really all I am. Or all I was."

"You're still hers," she said, caressing my cheek. "Just like I'm still Daddy's girl and Momma's little helper. Nothing can change what we were to them or what they were to us. Nothing. If I never learn anything else from their deaths, I've learned that life goes on. You don't really understand that phrase until you've lived through what we have."

"That's so true. When she took her last breath, I wasn't sure if I could take another breath without her. I wasn't sure I even wanted to. But it came anyway. And I kept waking up each day. I ate. I bathed. I got dressed. Each and every day. And I kept on going even though I wasn't sure how I was doing it. I kept on going and, eventually, I realized that life had kept going somehow. She was no longer with me, but I kept going, and I could keep living, moving forward."

"I'm sure she's so proud of what you have made of yourself."

Looking at her sweet face, I knew that even though she had a ways to go, her mother and father were smiling down on her too. Running my fingertips over her cheek, I whispered, "Your mom and dad are extremely proud of you and how strong you've turned out to be. You can do anything, you know. You have gone through the worst and still came out on top. Don't let anyone hold you back, Millie."

The world is yours for the taking. Just grab hold of what's yours now.

Chapter Eight

Millie

Soft music filtered into my mind as I took a deep breath. "Hmm," I moaned, stretching my arms and legs.

The sheet stuck to my inner thigh, and I tugged at it, pulling it away from my skin. An uncomfortable burning sensation followed, and I moved my leg, which proved painful as well.

What the hell is going on?

My body woke up in slow waves. First, pain and stiffness in my nether regions concerned me. Slowly, I moved my hand under the blanket, running it over my stomach and down between my legs, finding a sticky mess. My time of the month wasn't for two more weeks, so I had no idea why I would be sticky down there.

Pulling my hand back out from under the blanket, I opened my eyes to look at it.

No blood?

"Umph." The sound came from the end of the bed.

Sitting up, I looked at the end of the bed. Swallowing hard, I saw the figure of a tall man lying in my bed. Only his head was at the other end and when I looked to my left, there was a foot resting on the pillow.

No! No! No!

Squeezing my eyes tightly shut, I tried to wake myself up. This had to be a horrible nightmare. I couldn't have brought a man home with me. I did not do things like that.

It had been ages since I'd had sex. I was too tired for sex. I was too busy working and trying to raise my sister to have sex. I wasn't emotionally available enough to have sex.

When I opened my eyes, I couldn't bring myself to look at the lump of the man in my bed. Whoever it was, there had to be some problem with whoever I'd gone and done the nasty with.

I didn't have the time for a boyfriend. I didn't have the want-to for one either. And if this guy was from Shiner, then I would have to see him all the time. That meant things could turn bad if he wanted more than just sex from me.

He might want a relationship!

Not only did I not want to be in a relationship, but I also didn't want to have to talk about why I didn't want to be in one. That was the main reason I hadn't had sex in such a long time.

There was a time in my life when men only wanted to hit it and quit it. And my heart had been broken more than once by guys like that. But after my parents' deaths, when I had already lost too much of myself, all I wanted was a guy who wanted to hit it and quit it.

I had tried it twice. Each time, I'd hurt the guys when I had to let them know that I didn't want any sort of relationship at all. I'd only wanted sex from them. And the way they had looked at me, their eyes filled with hurt, had made me feel so bad for what I'd done that I just hadn't done it again.

Until last night.

Now, there was some man in my bed—a bed I couldn't get up and run away from. He would wake up, and then there would be a lot of awkwardness. I wouldn't come right out and say that I had a good time, thank you, but now get the fuck out of my house and don't ever come back.

For one, I had no idea if I'd had a good time or not. I didn't remember anything.

Eyes closed, I tried to recollect the events that had led up to my current situation. There was the slow dancing with the rich guy from out of town.

I couldn't believe the smile that moved my lips as I remembered Jag's super-hot face looking down into mine as we held each other, moving fluidly together, forgetting about everyone else in the bar.

Damn, that man is fine!

Despite how good-looking Jag was, the way he smelled like fine leather and expensive cologne, and as good as I felt in his strong arms, I was sure that I hadn't brought him back to my apartment, which was more like a shack than a real home. Even if I was super drunk, I wouldn't have wanted him to see where I lived.

He was rich. Surely, I would've felt too ashamed for him to see the way I lived. Surely, I wouldn't have asked him to come home with me. But I must have asked someone to come home with me. Otherwise, I would be alone now instead of trying my best not to freak the fuck out.

The weird thing was that I only remembered Jag. Dancing with him. And then he was looking into my eyes. His blue eyes were shining brightly, and then he leaned in closer and closer until something remarkable happened.

Fireworks!

The kiss came flooding back to my memory, and my lips actually tingled as I relived the moment in my mind. It was the softest kiss I'd ever had, and then it grew deeper. I'd felt that kiss all the way to my bones. My entire body lit up with so much more than desire. I needed the man.

I saw my hand in his. I walked in front of him, pulling him to come with me somewhere. Suddenly, we were on the sidewalk outside the bar. My back was against the brick wall, and his mouth crashed onto mine.

One of his hands slid up my leg, under my skirt, resting on my hip as he pressed his body against mine, pinning me to the wall. I wrapped my legs around him, my body pulsing with the need for so much more.

The next thing I recalled was running with him, our hands clasped tightly as I led the way down the sidewalk, then up the street, and finally all the way to my apartment.

Dear God, I dragged him home with me!

We had barely gotten inside when I began undressing him. Jag's eyes were on my breasts as he pulled my shirt off over my head. He quickly unclasped my bra, setting them free. Then he gathered me in his arms, lifting me up. Taking one breast into his hot mouth, he sucked and nipped at it, driving me mad with lust and desire as I ran my hands through his thick, dark, wavy hair.

Opening my eyes, I found myself breathing hard with just the memory of what had gone on the night before. Not wanting to wake Jag up, I tried getting myself back under control.

God only knew what I looked like. My curly hair surely resembled a bird's nest by now. If I had just straightened it, then it wouldn't have been so unruly. But I'd listened to my little sister and left it in its natural state. Which was great—until I slept on it.

I had to ease out of the bed so as not to wake him. It was bad enough that I'd brought him to my crappy apartment, but I couldn't let him see me like this. Plus, I needed a shower.

Thankfully, I made it out, and he still lay in a heap on the bed. Our clothes lay everywhere around the room, and since the bedroom door had remained open, I could see into the living room. My panties were hanging from the ceiling fan.

I wasn't going to let him wake up and see something like that, so I walked out of the room and jumped up, grabbing them. Then I found my bra near the front door, which I now noticed hadn't even been locked.

Good Lord, we could've been murdered in our sleep!

It was obvious to me that I could not let myself go and get so relaxed ever again. I had no sense at all when I wasn't trying to be responsible. Bringing a stranger home with me. Having sex with him. Leaving the door unlocked. I'd made every wrong decision a person could make.

The one thing I was glad of was that Jag wasn't going to be staying in town. No matter what, I wouldn't have to worry about him trying to become my boyfriend. I wouldn't have to hurt him in any way because he was leaving town, maybe even that very day.

Knowing that, I relaxed a little. There wasn't any reason to worry about anything now. I would have our one night of memories to keep me warm for a long time.

After locking the door, I leaned back against it, remembering how he'd pushed me up against it, kissing me hard, my naked breasts smashed against his naked chest.

The man was built like a Greek god. There wasn't even a centimeter of fat on him. Every part of him was hard as a rock. Like he was made out of marble or something.

Running my hands down my body, I recalled the way his hands had moved all over it—caressing, squeezing, playing with parts of me in ways I hadn't known would feel so damn good.

Tiptoeing back into the bedroom, I put the clothes I'd picked up off the floor of my apartment into a single pile on the bedroom floor. Mine were all entangled with his, and it reminded me of how our bodies had each wrapped around the other's—refusing to let even an inch separate us.

We'd gone at it like a couple of sex-starved monkeys. It had me wondering how long it had been since he'd had sex. A gorgeous man like him probably didn't have any trouble at all getting women into bed.

He had seemed equally as ravenous for me as I was for him, though. Maybe making money took a lot of his time. Maybe he didn't have sex a whole lot the way I thought he must have. Maybe he and I were a lot more alike than I had initially thought.

I had gotten the impression that making money was the top thing on both of our minds. Only he was obviously much better at making money than I was.

He'd given me some good advice too, telling me not to let anyone hold me back. Of course, I didn't know if anyone was holding me back at all. Well, maybe I was doing that to myself, but I had to give Myra the chance to become something before I took the time it would take to make something of myself.

Sacrifice was part of being a parent. And I was the closest thing to a parent to Myra. So, sacrifices had to be made. But one day it would be my turn.

Trying to be as quiet as a mouse, I pulled my robe off the hook on my door and went to the bathroom across the hall to shower. I pulled the door halfway closed but didn't shut it all the way because it would make a loud squeaking noise that would probably wake up Jag. And I didn't want him to wake just yet.

Looking into the bathroom mirror, I gasped at the way my hair looked—smooshed on one side and standing nearly straight up on the other. I had to get it washed and quick.

It didn't matter that I would most likely never see Jag again. I didn't want him to see me looking like something the cat had dug up, chewed on, and then spit out before dragging it into the house.

After a hurried shower, I draped my robe around me, put my washed hair into a towel to let it absorb most of the moisture, then picked up my toothbrush. My mouth tasted super nasty.

But as I thought about that, my mind traveled back in time to all the kissing Jag and I had done and how yummy all those kisses had been.

I knew that I would eventually be able to remember everything we'd done that night. I'd only had three beers before he showed up at the bar. Once he got there, neither of us drank very much of the beers Rachel had brought us. We were too busy kissing and dancing to do much drinking.

And there had been laughing too. Some talking. Some nuzzling. Lots of things going on to keep our mouths much too busy to drink. I had to smile as I thought about all the things he and I had done.

He'd given me enough memories to last a long, long time. My entire body began tingling as I pictured him between my legs, moving like waves over my body. The man knew how to move. He knew exactly the right places to touch me.

Sex had never been that good before, not even with guys I'd dated for a while. Jag just knew how to push all the right buttons on my body by pure instinct.

Smiling away, I knew it was best that he wasn't going to be around for long. This way, there would only be great memories of our night together. Nothing bad could mess up the perfection of the night we'd had.

Pulling the towel off my head, I let my curls fall as I looked at myself in the mirror. I was glowing. Like, super radiant.

Multiple orgasms are great for the complexion.

I hoped the glow would last a while before it faded with work, anxiety about being able to pay our bills, and all the other crap that made up my life.

But for now, I looked better than I had ever looked. I had never thought of myself as beautiful, but at that moment I felt gorgeous, and the reflection that looked back at me told me that I was.

Who knew that great sex could actually change the way a person looked?

Since I'd never had sex that amazing before, I'd had no idea that it could make such a physical impact on a person. It made me wonder how I would end up looking and acting if Jag did stay around and we had lots more sex.

Shaking my head, I squeezed some toothpaste onto my toothbrush. I couldn't even let myself think like that. He had to leave. He was a busy man, I was sure. He wouldn't have time for me. And I didn't have time for him either.

Best not to even think about us having time for each other. It's never going to happen anyway.

Chapter Nine

Jag

Waking to the feel of myself laying on a lumpy mattress, I smiled, recalling the reason for it. "Mmmm. Millie." Rolling onto my back, I found myself turned the wrong way in the small bed—my feet on the pillow, my head at the end of the bed. And Millie not in the bed at all.

The night had been very good to us. Passions in overdrive, we'd spent the better part of the night wrapped up in each other in the best ways. I couldn't remember ever having anything close to the experiences we'd shared.

The only thing I felt bad about was the fact that I had to leave town soon. But I could always come back, and she could always come to see me. Not that I was about to start pushing her for more than she was ready for. But God knew I was already ready for more of what she had to offer. "Millie?" Wrapping the sheet around my waist, I got out of bed.

"In here," she said.

Looking out of the bedroom door that was halfway open, I spotted her in the bathroom across the hallway, brushing her teeth. "Morning, hot stuff."

She leaned over and spit the toothpaste out before using a hand towel to wipe her mouth. "Morning to you too, super stud."

The woman glowed in a way that took my breath away. Moving in behind her, I wrapped my arms around her waist, resting my chin on her shoulder as I looked at our reflections in the mirror. "Don't we make a great-looking couple?"

A blush covered her cheeks. "Come on, now." She turned in my arms, slipping her hands around my back. "Last night was fun."

"Last night was more than just fun. At least, to me it was." Leaning in close, I went for a kiss.

Her finger between our lips got in my way. "We can't get this going again, Jag. My little sister could be here any minute, and I don't want her to know what I've done. You know, bringing a man home. I'm trying to set a good example for her."

"How old is she?"

"Sixteen."

"Oh, yeah. You don't want her to think that this is okay." I let her go and went back to the bedroom. "I'll just find my clothes. Any idea where they all got to?"

"I've gathered them up and piled them in a corner in the bedroom." She turned and moved in front of me, back toward the bedroom. "They're all mixed up with mine. Let me get them for you."

"Wanna go grab some breakfast?"

Bending over to get the clothes, her ass looked great even under the thin robe she wore. "If I didn't have Myra—that's my sister—to think about, I would love to go to breakfast with you. But I should have it with her."

"Yeah, you're right." She tossed me my jeans, and I caught them in one hand. "I can see the responsible side of you has come back out."

Turning to face me, she held out the rest of my clothes. "I know, this side of me isn't nearly as attractive as the fun side I showed you last night. But this is who I am most of the time. That girl you got to see last night barely ever shows her face."

Throwing my things on the bed, I took her hands, pulling her to me until our bodies were flush. "I'd like to see a hell of a lot more of that part of you, Millie."

Blinking, she looked into my eyes. "Jag, last night was a thing I will never regret."

"I sense a *but* coming." And I didn't like where this seemed to be going.

"*But*, you and I are very different people. Besides that, you know that I'm not really in the right spot in my life to do much other than work. At least, right now that's the case. Give me five or six years and see where I'm at then. I mean—I'll be here in Shiner, of course."

"And why is that, Millie?"

"This is my hometown."

"I've got two hometowns. Wyoming, New York, and Modesto, California. Two very different places. I live in neither one anymore."

"Is there really a place called Wyoming, New York?"

"There is. It is small and beautiful. Especially during the winter months."

"Why did you leave if it was beautiful?"

"My mother wanted to leave, and I was a kid who had no say in the matter. But that's not the point. The point I'm trying to make is that you can live anywhere you want. You don't have to be stuck in one place."

"Easy for you to say. You've got the money to move around the whole world freely. I don't have enough money to get out of town. Much less get myself another place to live. And where would I go anyway?"

"I don't know. Where have you always wanted to go?"

Raised brows told me she might not have ever considered that before. "When we were young, our parents took us to a zoo in Dallas. We drove through all these different towns on the way there. Austin was a nightmare. The traffic was so backed up that it took my dad nearly three hours to get through it. But once the traffic thinned out a bit, the scenery was pretty. I liked this one town called Round Rock. But what would I be able to do there?"

"Anything you want, I would guess. You're a waitress, and that means you can get a job pretty much anywhere."

"Yeah, but I wouldn't know anyone. I count on these people, Jag. Myra is the only family I've got. It's the friends we grew up with who are our family now. Why would we leave them?"

"I guess I'm wrong, Millie. Maybe you should stay where you feel the safest. Who am I to tell you how to live?"

"No, I get it. I should have some dreams. I should want more. I just can't really want anything for myself right now."

Kissing the top of her head, I knew I had to shut the hell up. She had a lot going on, and I had no idea what was right or wrong in her life. She had to do what her gut told her to do. And that was that she needed to get her sister off to a good start in life, and then she'd get her start. If that ever came for her. "You do what you have to do, Millie."

Pushing me away from her gently, she asked, "So, what are your plans for the day?"

"I'm going to the brewery to check things out. I might want to invest in it. I've got an idea about taking the marketing to Germany to see what kinds of sales can be made there."

"Why?"

"Why not? I mean, the extra sales would help the company. And the company is the heart of this small town, right? Wouldn't the success of the brewery help the town and its people?"

"I guess you're right."

"Anyway, I'm not sure if I want to invest yet. And I'm not sure the owners will even let me. So, we'll see what happens." I had to get going. There was a lot to do, and I'd spent the prior day playing around. Now, it was time to get to work. "I'm going to borrow your bathroom, get dressed, then I'll get out of here."

"Yeah." She nodded then sat on the bed as I left the room.

As I got dressed, I wondered about her and what could happen if we didn't have to part ways. I moved around a lot, staying busy. That kept me from forming any real bonds with any of the women I'd dated. With Millie, I had the feeling that we had already bonded.

We shared something that I hadn't shared with anyone before—the common element of having both lost our parents. At least she had her sister. I had no one. Being all alone in the world wasn't easy.

Millie had her hometown and the people she'd known her whole life. And it occurred to me that I had chosen to do much the same as she had. I'd stayed close to my mom's best friend—so close that I'd hired her to be my personal and professional assistant. So, I knew why Millie wanted to stay right where she was and had always been. I'd done something sort of like that myself.

When I came out of the bathroom, I found Millie fully dressed, sitting in the living room with a cup of steaming hot coffee between her hands. "Glad to see you dressed. Care to walk me to the main street? I don't want to get lost on my way back to the RV park."

"Yeah, I'll walk with you." Putting the cup down, she got up, and we walked out the door.

I took her hand in mine as we walked side by side. "I don't want you to think that last night wasn't special to me, Millie."

"It was to me too." She leaned her head on my shoulder. "You have left me with some awesome memories, Jag."

"You've left me with some too, hot stuff."

"No one has ever called me that before." She laughed a little. "I kind of like it."

"I'm only stating the truth. You are one hot girl, Millie."

"You are the one who brought that out in me. No one else ever has, that's for sure."

"Good to hear." I didn't want to think about her being with anyone else. "You know, this doesn't have to be a one-time thing."

"Let's not go there, Jag. I like that we're parting on good terms. No bad feelings between us. You know?"

"Yes, I get it. But that doesn't mean that we can't stay in touch and see each other every now and then."

"It won't be easy. I'm not one to sit and talk on the phone. And my schedule is chaotic, to say the least. I work as much as they'll let me. And when I'm not working, I'm helping my sister with homework, doing laundry, or cleaning the apartment. There's always something that needs to be done."

"Okay, I won't bring it up anymore. If we meet again, then we meet again. If that's how you want it."

"Yes, that is exactly how I want it."

"So, you're not going to give me your number, is what you're saying," I said, knowing she wasn't about to give me a way to contact her. I could feel it in her vibe. Whatever happened or didn't happen between us was going to be left up to chance. I wasn't super cool with it, but I had to respect what she wanted.

"That's right."

"Do you still have mine? Or did you throw it away?"

"I've got it. I'm not going to use it, though. So, don't go waiting for a call to come. I'm probably going to toss it anyway. Just to be sure that I don't get all into my feelings and call you sometime."

"But you can if you want to. I'm not nearly as busy as you are. I'm free to talk whenever you want. Don't toss my number, is what I'm trying to say here." I wanted there to be some way to connect if she ever really wanted to.

Shrugging, she said, "I don't know. I'll think about it. I'm not promising anything, though."

"Yeah, I can see that you don't like to make promises, Millie."

"Oh, I make plenty of them, Jag. I promised to take care of my sister, and that's my number one priority." She stopped as we stepped onto the sidewalk lining the main street. "I think you can make it back to the RV park from here, Jag."

I didn't want to let go of her hand and held tightly to it. "It's pretty dead here this morning."

"It'll liven up around noon." She looked at our clasped hands. "Are you planning on letting my hand go?" Her eyes moved up to meet mine.

"So, this is it then?" I asked. "No breakfast together?"

She shook her head. "No. Thank you for asking, though. You're a nice guy, Jag. I'm glad we got to know each other. You won't be forgotten."

"Neither will you." I didn't want to walk away from her at all. "How about lunch? I'll take you and your sister to lunch. Anywhere you want."

"You've got the brewery thing to do. Do what you came here to do. Don't let me get in your way. I wasn't the reason why you came here. Remember that you have a goal here, and I wasn't any part of that. Stay the course, Jag."

"Jag Briggs," I said. "Remember my whole name just in case you ever want to look me up on social media or anything. I've got homes in Dallas, Los Angeles, and New York. My social media profile says that Los Angeles is where I'm from, though. You can instant message me if you ever lose my number. So, what about your social media info?"

"I'm not on it. There's no time for anything like that."

"No way, Millie. Everyone is on some type of social media platform. Don't try to bullshit me."

"Not me, Jag. Let's not make this awkward or weird or anything that will take away from the night we had. So, see you if I see you, Jag Briggs."

"Millie?" I asked. I felt a lump beginning to form in my throat, and I hated the way it felt.

"Yes."

"What's your last name? Just in case you do ever get on social media."

"Powers."

"Okay. If you ever do get on social media and I send you a friend request, you had better accept it."

"I won't—but okay."

"Promise?"

"I promise. And I don't break promises. But don't go holding your breath. I don't have time for things like that." She tugged her hand, and I had to let it go. "Thank you."

"Just so you know, I'm only letting you go because I respect the shit out of you."

"Thank you. I respect you too. Keep doing you, Jag. It's worked great so far. And I'm sure it always will."

"Yeah, so far it's worked out for me. And you make sure you take your turn when the time comes. Promise me—one day, you will do you, Millie Powers. I know you'll be great at whatever you decide to do."

"I promise you. One day, when it's my turn, I will do me, Jag. And thanks for believing in me. That means a lot. It really does." She looked over her shoulder, back the way we'd come. "I've got to go."

"Okay." I wanted to grab her, hold her, kiss her. But I knew that if I did that it would be impossible to let her go the way she wanted me to. "See you, Millie."

"Yeah, see ya, Jag." And then she walked away.

I watched her for a while before I turned around and walked away too. When a tear fell down my cheek, I quickly wiped it away.

That was the best night of my life, and now it's over.

Chapter Ten

Millie

Piling all the dirty laundry into the basket, I hauled it to the laundromat next door to the apartment complex. Rachel pulled up just as I got to the entrance. She honked the horn, laughing like she'd done something very funny. "I didn't expect to find you here, Millie."

Myra got out of the car, running to get the basket from me. "Here, I'll do this. Rachel told me you had a very fun night that went late. You can go back and rest if you want."

Looking at Rachel with my mouth ajar, I asked, "You told her?"

"Not everything." Rachel put her finger to her lips. "Come here, talk to me. The kids are sleeping in the back, so I can't get out."

Myra had already gone inside the laundromat, so I got into the passenger side of Rachel's car. Her kids were passed out in their car seats in the back. "I guess my sister let them stay up late."

With a shrug, she didn't seem like that mattered much to her. "So, tell me everything. Did you and Jag—well, you know?"

"I'm not about to tell you what we did or did not do." I smiled as I thought about it, though. "But it was insanely wonderful."

"I knew it," she said with a grin. "What now?"

"What do you mean by that?"

"Well, what are you and he going to do now? Are you going to see him today?"

"No."

"Why not?" She gasped. "Did he leave without saying goodbye or something like that?"

"Not at all. He wanted me to have breakfast with him. There was no way I was going to do that. Tongues would be wagging about me if we were seen out this morning."

"Tongues are going to wag anyway, Millie. You two were all over each other before you guys disappeared. You might as well see him today. Everyone's talking anyway."

"Well, if they see us out together, then they'll really talk. Anyway, I don't want to do that to him."

"Do what to him?" she asked with a puzzled expression.

"Make him think that we can have some sort of relationship when in reality, we can't."

"Why can't you?"

"He's a busy person, and so am I," I clarified, even though I thought it was obvious why it wouldn't work out for us.

"He's probably able to make his own schedule, and you're a waitress, for God's sakes. You've got time for a relationship, Millie. I'm a waitress, and I've had time for relationships."

Looking back at her kids, I nodded. "And look where that got you. I've got a handful of years left to put Myra before myself. You've got two decades."

"Hey, I love my kids."

"I know you do. But where are their fathers?"

She sighed heavily. "Yes, I know. In hindsight, it might not have been the best idea to start relationships with men who lived out of town."

"You think?" I'd seen many people in my small town fall for people who lived elsewhere. But long-distance relationships aren't easy, and most do not work out.

"I know you love your kids. So, you got something positive out of those relationships. But you also got a ton of heartache. Jag is the kind of man who would leave my heart in tatters if I let him in."

"You guys had some intense chemistry, Millie. I haven't seen anything like that before. I wouldn't be so quick to blow him off if I were you."

"I've got more self-discipline than you do, Rachel. You have no idea how unprepared I am for any sort of romantic relationship. Even if Jag is better than anyone I've ever met."

"He was magnificent in bed, wasn't he?"

"Come on, Rachel." I didn't want to talk about how great he was. But then again, I couldn't really help myself. "What do you think?"

"I knew it!"

"I've got great memories about him. No regrets at all. And I want to keep things that way."

"So, you think that never seeing him again is better than making some more memories with him?" She shook her head. "No way, Millie. You're crazy. Take what you can out of that man."

"No." I wasn't going to do anything like that. "Rachel, he's sensitive. I can't hurt him the way I know I would if we tried to make things work."

"Why would you hurt him?"

"I don't have time for him, is why."

"Make time for him. How hard could it be?"

"I can't do that. I've got to work."

"Stop hiding behind that. You can't just do everything for your sister and never do anything for yourself."

"I did something for myself last night. And that will keep me content for a good long time. All the memories are good ones. I'll take that over some long-distance relationship that turns stagnant."

"I can't believe that anything could possibly go stagnant with a man like Jag."

"I would be willing to bet that you are wrong. If I had the money to make bets—which I don't. I'm not saying that I would get bored with him. He would definitely get bored with me, though. For now, he thinks I'm hot stuff and I would like to keep it that way."

"Hot stuff?" she asked with a grin. "He said that?"

"He did. And with him, I have to agree that I was hot stuff. But I can't keep that up. You know that about me. I'm tired all the time. And I do get testy sort of often."

"I chalk the testiness up to the lack of sex you get."

"It's not that."

"I think it is that. Have you looked at yourself in a mirror today? You're glowing. Sex looks good on you."

I knew I looked exceptionally good. "Yeah, I saw that too. But it can't last. Nothing like this," I cradled my face, "can last."

"I'm not so sure about that."

"I am."

"Anyway, you still have his phone number in case you change your mind. But you should probably let him have yours too. It's only fair."

"No." I wasn't going to give him so much access to me. "He knows where I'll be if he wants to see me. It's not like I'm going anywhere, and he knows that."

"So, that's what you're doing," she said with a nod.

"What are you talking about?"

"You're waiting to see if he comes back here to see you and how often he does that. I get it now. You could've just told me that, Millie. It's a good test to see how much he really wants a relationship with you."

"I'm not testing him. I honestly hope he doesn't come back here. That might mess up the great memories I have of him. You know, if we argue, it will taint my memories."

"You two did argue. Like right off the bat, you argued. So, you most definitely can argue and then make up. If that's what you're worried about, don't."

"I'm not worried about anything. For the first time in a long time, I'm not worried about a damn thing. And it's all because of the night we had. So, leave me alone about stuff. I'm happy. Can't you be happy for me too?"

"You're happy right now. But what about when the afterglow wears off and you find yourself alone again?"

"I'll have my memories to keep me company. And you can trust me when I say that these memories are so hot that they're sure to warm me back up if I begin to feel the chill of loneliness."

"You will ache for more. I'm telling you the truth, Millie. Your body is going to crave more of what that man can give you."

"Nah." I didn't believe her at all. "Not me."

"Any person who looks like you do right now—all glowing with life and fulfillment—would want more when the glow begins to wear off. You'll need another dose of what gave that to you in the first place. And you might try to find that with some other guy. But I can promise you that you won't find it."

"I agree with you on that. Jag is the only one who instantly knew where and how to touch me. And I'm thankful for our night together. But that's all I can have. For now. If we're supposed to be together then when I can do me, he'll be there. If not, then he won't."

"You are talking about years, Millie. It will be years before you'll allow yourself to do you. You've said it too many times. Myra will have to be out of college and making her own living before you begin to do you."

"It will be years. How can I expect Jag or anyone to wait for me when I've got so much on my plate? The answer is that I can't expect him to do that."

"But you should at least give him the chance to make that decision for himself. What if he's happy with whatever free time you can give him? What if he has more patience than you think he does? What if you two could have some sort of relationship while you're waiting for your sister to get her life going?"

Sitting there, I wondered if Rachel was right.

Maybe we could just see how things go.

"I don't know."

"You won't know until you talk to him."

"And if he doesn't want to do that? I mean, that might crush me. No, it *will* crush me. I can't put myself at risk like that. Right now, I've left things on a high note. If I give him to chance to turn me down, then I'll be torn apart."

"You're a chicken, is what you are," she said with a smirk. "A coward. Afraid of your own shadow."

"No, I'm not." Opening the car door, I realized that I had to at least talk to Jag.

"Where are you going?"

"To see Jag. I'm not going to let him leave without hearing out what he wants first. I'm not saying that I'll agree to anything. But he has feelings too, and I would be wrong to not give him a chance to express them."

"Good. I'm glad you're thinking about more than just yourself."

"It's probably a bad idea, but I'm going to go over to his RV and give him the chance to tell me what he wants. And I hope that when I turn him down, it doesn't hurt him."

"You shouldn't just turn him down, Millie. Give yourself some time to think about things. You don't have to do it alone all the time. No one ever said you had to do that."

"It's just easier this way." Walking away from her car, I wasn't sure if I was doing the smartest thing. We'd parted ways amicably, and what I was about to do might screw that up. But I had to do it anyway.

On the way over, I almost stopped five times, thinking that this was a mistake and I needed to turn around and go back home. But something made me keep going each time. And the next thing I knew, my fist was bouncing off the door to his RV and the door came open.

An older woman stood there, looking at me. "Can I help you?"

"I'm Millie. Is Jag here?"

"No." She stepped outside, closing the door behind her. "So you're the one he spent the night with."

"He told you about that?" I found that rather shocking.

"Yes. Jag and I are very close. He tells me everything."

"I'm sorry. He hasn't told me anything about you. You are?"

"I'm Samantha Petty, his assistant. And he's told me everything about you, Millie Powers."

That was a good sign. "Does he talk to you about all the girls he's interested in?"

"Let's not go there. See, the thing is that you aren't in his league. You know that, though. You did the right thing when you told him that it's best for you two to part ways without trying to stay connected by anything."

"I know he's got money and I've got very little. But I'm not really out of his league. He and I have a lot in common. Did he tell you that?"

"That doesn't matter at all. You are never leaving this town, and Jag's future is in world travel. You would be out of your comfort zone, to say the least."

"I can't travel anywhere while I'm still taking care of my sister."

"That's what I'm saying. You can't be what he needs. You've got your things to do, and he's got his. Your worlds collided only briefly. Be happy with what you got from him but don't expect anything more. If not for his sake, then for your own. You don't know him the way I do—he's sure to break your heart. It sounds like your heart isn't in the best of shape after losing your parents. If I were you, I wouldn't test it."

"Why are you so sure he would break my heart?" I didn't think he was a bad guy at all.

"I've known him for many years. I've seen him in action. He's never stayed in a relationship for more than a month or two. His mind moves fast. He's into one thing and then on to another before you know it. It's just who he is. We're leaving here today. He's set up a meeting in San Antonio for tonight. If he was as into you as you think he is, then why would he want to leave this town so quickly?"

She was right. "I see." I knew it had been stupid of me to go against what my gut had told me to do in the first place. "Well, I wish him well. Can you tell him that for me?"

"Honestly, it's best if you don't think about him anymore. Enjoy your memories. But don't think anything more will come of that one night. His mind is already moving on, and it hasn't been but a few hours since you two parted company. Best you do that too, dear."

I knew this was going to be a mistake. Stupid Rachel!

Chapter Eleven

Jag

"I'll meet you at the Menger Hotel at eight tonight. I look forward to seeing you and your wife, and I hope we can make each other some money." I stepped into the RV, happy that I'd been able to get a meeting with the owners of the brewery so easily.

Putting the phone into my back pocket, I saw that Miss Petty and Tex had already gotten the RV ready to go. "We're ready as soon as you are, Jag," she said. "Tex has things packed up, and he's ready to pull out."

"I've got one thing to do, and then we can be on our way." I wasn't going to leave town without talking to Millie one more time. "I just came by here first so that I could grab something."

"And where is it that you're going, Jag?" Miss Petty asked.

"To see Millie. I want to give her a picture of me, so she won't forget about me. She's trying to be strong, pretending she doesn't need anyone. I know she can make it all on her own, but I also know that she doesn't have to." I carried a picture of my mother and me everywhere I went. I'd put one in a frame to keep in the RV for when I traveled. I could make myself another copy, so I took the photo out of the frame and cut my mother out of the picture, putting that part in my wallet to keep. Then I placed the piece with only me in it back into the frame.

Miss Petty leaned against the wall near the door, looking at me with sadness in her eyes. "Jag, you shouldn't do that. You told me that she didn't want to keep in touch. She wants the memory of you, but she doesn't want *you*. She will never leave this town. You said so yourself. Once you've got this deal in the bag, we're going to travel to Germany. We'll be there for months."

Standing there, I didn't know what to say. But then I found the words, "She's just putting on a brave front. I know she is. I just want to leave her a reminder of me. That's all."

"Why?" she asked. "So she can look at that picture and think about you? So she can feel bad about herself for not being able to go with you? She's got real responsibilities here, Jag. It's not fair of you to flaunt your freedom when she's so utterly trapped right here in this small town. You are better than that.

Spending any more time with that girl would only hurt her. And you know that too. Don't be that selfish. You know your mother would give you the same advice."

Taking a seat on the sofa, I looked at the framed picture in my hand. "Maybe you're right. Maybe she should just forget about me."

Miss Petty sat next to me, patting me on the knee. "Girls like that end up staying at the same job they had when they were in high school. They end up marrying someone they went to school with and have known their whole lives. They don't travel the globe. They don't advance in their career. They just live day to day, paycheck to paycheck, and never strive for more."

I did not want to think of Millie that way. "She's going to do more with her life. She just needs time for her sister to get out on her own so that she can find her way."

"She'll find another local. They will get married, buy one of the homes here that have been around for years, and they'll have kids of their own. And those kids will do the same things as them. It's a never-ending circle of life in small towns like these. I'm sorry, Jag. These are just the facts. Leave without seeing her—it's best for you both."

Maybe she's right.

"There's something special about her."

"No, there's not. You've never met someone like her, is all."

"You're right. I have never met anyone like her."

"She's got values that you respect. She's taken the roles of both parents so that her sister can make something of herself. That's noble. Admirable. And attractive too. You saw all those things in her, and you liked them."

"There was more, though. It wasn't just those things."

"Yes, she must've been very pretty too. But none of that really matters because her place is here, and yours is everywhere else but here."

"Who's to say that I can't buy a home or build a home right here?" I could do whatever I put my mind to. "If she and I are meant to be, then I can make this place my home too. If that's the way she wants to live her life, I can adapt."

"Why should you?" She laughed as if what she'd said was funny. "Why should you stop living life the way you want just so that girl can continue to live life the way she wants? How fair is that to you, Jag?"

"I'm happy wherever I am." That was true. "I can be happy anywhere."

"You're jumping ahead in this timeline of you and this small-town girl. You have no idea if you two would even work out. Most couples don't work out when they live far apart or one of them has to travel a lot for work. In the end, both of you will be hurt. Trust me. Things are best left this way."

She had a point. She had many of them. But my heart was begging me to take a chance. And maybe I could take the pain of rejection if it came to it. Despite that, I had to think about Millie too.

I had to travel for the next few months—even longer if we made a deal on the brewery investment. It wouldn't be right of me to leave Millie with the idea that we had a chance of being more to each other right away.

For now, I wouldn't be around. My future plans would have me traveling places where I would have to stay to make things happen. But the fact was that I didn't *have* to do any of it.

I had more money than any one person would ever need. I didn't have to make these investments in small-town businesses. But it was something I'd dreamt about doing for a while.

One night of crazy passion with a woman who had a hell of a lot going on in her life wasn't worth putting off all my plans. If Millie and I were meant to be, then life would bring us back together in some way.

I had to go on and do the things I'd planned on doing. And I had to leave Millie right where she was. She was happy here too. This was all she'd ever known. She would be fine. I would be fine.

But how happy will I be?

Would it be possible for me to focus as well as I had before meeting her? Would I be as successful in my work as I'd been before her?

My mind was caught on her. Somehow, she had taken hold of my heart in such a small amount of time.

That sounds insane.

"Yeah, let's get rolling. I'm being stupid about this. She's just a girl. I've been alone too long. I've got to get out more. I'm spending too much time on my computer, picking the best stocks, researching companies. Now and then, I'll need you to remind me that I need to get out and ask a girl on a date. Secluding myself isn't working for me anymore. It's making me think I'm falling in love with a complete stranger—which is just crazy."

"It is crazy," Miss Petty agreed with a smile and a pat on my back. "You can't fall in love with someone so quickly. And you can't change all your plans for anyone so quickly either. You have big things ahead of you, Jag. Don't let anyone get in your way."

Sitting there, her words rang in my ears. *Don't let anyone get in your way.*

I had said the same thing to Millie the night before. It was obvious that I needed to take my own advice. "You're right, Miss Petty. Investing in small-town America is an important undertaking. I can't just change my mind about what has been calling to me for over a year now."

"Good. I'm glad you came around." She got up and went to the front of the RV. "Tex, we are ready to head out to San Antonio."

"You got it, Miss Petty." The RV roared to life, taking me away from Shiner—away from Millie.

I went back to the bedroom. I didn't want to be around anyone. It might have been the right thing to do—leaving without saying anything to her—but it hurt nonetheless.

Looking out the window above the bed, I watched as we left the town behind us. In my imagination, I saw Millie running into the street, waving wildly, screaming for me to come back to her. But none of it was real.

She was probably home, cleaning her house or doing some other mundane chore of which she said she had so many. Or maybe she was sleeping soundly in the bed we'd made love in all night long. Whatever she was doing, she was doing it without me.

Why I longed for her so much was a mystery to me. I'd never felt this way before. Sadness had wrapped its solid fist around my heart, and I wasn't sure if I could figure out how to break its icy grip. I wasn't even sure if I wanted to try.

Turning to lie on my back, I closed my eyes, allowing my mind to drift back to the night before.

Her body underneath mine. Her wrists in my hand as I moved above her. Her beautiful face gazing up at me. The softness of her flesh as I slid my body up and down hers, reminding me of silky sheets caressing my skin. The firmness of her breasts against my bare chest. The way she breathed slowly once she'd fallen asleep in my arms. The way I kissed her awake so that we could make love again. All wonderful memories that I prayed would never fade away.

Getting up, I reached into the laundry bin, pulling out the shirt I'd worn to the bar. Burying my nose in it, I inhaled deeply and found that her sweet scent still lingered.

Cuddling with it on the bed, I knew I would never wash that shirt again. That was all I had to remember her by. I didn't ever want to forget Millie Powers—even if we never saw each other again. I never wanted to forget her or what we had for that one night.

Falling asleep, I found her there in my dreams. Her smile pulled me to her. We danced in the sunlight, holding each other, vowing to never let go.

Her heart was beating so loudly that I heard it and pressed my ear against her chest. "It beats for me, doesn't it, Millie?"

"Only for you, Jag." Laughing, she moved in circles, and I moved with her. "I'm so glad you stayed with me."

"Where else would I be?" Looking into her brown eyes, I saw my life in them.

"We will stay here, and we will always be happy," she whispered. "All I need is you, Jag."

"All I need is you too, Millie. Only you. Wherever you are, that's where I'll be. No matter where you go, I'll be there."

"I'm not leaving, Jag."

My eyes fluttered open as the RV came to a stop. I sat up in bed, blinking, trying to pull myself out of the dream. It had felt so real. But it wasn't real at all.

Getting up, I went to the bathroom and splashed water on my face, then looked in the mirror. "You can't act like this. You don't even know her. She's not your life. You've made a life for yourself already. Stop being a puss."

A knock came on the door. "Jag, you okay in there?" Miss Petty asked.

"Yeah, I'm okay."

"I heard you talking. Anyway, we're in San Antonio. You slept the whole way. I'm about to go into the office and check us in for the night. Tex will stay with the RV. You and I will be picked up and taken to the hotel. I've already booked us two rooms there for tonight. So, pack a bag, okay?"

"Yeah, I'll do that."

"Okay. I'll be right back. I've got a car coming for us already, so get ready."

"Yeah." Wiping my face, I knew I had no choice but to get my shit together and quick. I could not meet the owners of the brewery acting like a love-struck pup. "Get it together, man."

"What?" she asked.

"Nothing." I opened the bathroom door. "You can go and check-in. I'll pack my bag."

"You seem a little out of it," she said. "Maybe take some vitamins or something."

"Good idea." I went to the bedroom to pack a bag.

Whatever this feeling was, I had to shake it off. It wasn't a healthy feeling at all. It reminded me of when we found out that my mother had cancer. Like I didn't know what was going to happen. And then the worst happened.

I didn't like feeling this way. I knew I had to snap out of it. Life wasn't meant to be lived in a daze. I knew that. I'd lived that way for a long time. But I wasn't going back there.

Millie was in the past. I had to leave her there. No more dreaming about her. No more fantasizing about her. I couldn't let any thoughts about her come to my mind anymore.

She was like something I could become addicted to—and becoming addicted to anything was not good. I had to get my head back in my own game.

Half an hour later, I was packed and ready to go. I walked out of the RV, and soon the car pulled up to pick us up. I got in first as Miss Petty was still packing her bag. "How far is the Menger Hotel?" I asked the driver just to make small talk.

"About fifteen minutes. You know that place is haunted, right?" he said as he looked at me through the rearview mirror.

I just laughed. "No, I didn't know that."

No need to worry, I'm a little haunted myself.

Chapter Twelve

Millie

Why did I listen to Rachel?

I'd felt pretty great before going to see Jag. Then his stupid assistant had to go and ruin everything. And the worst part was that I had known something like that would happen.

If I hadn't listened to my friend, then I wouldn't be in such a shitty mood. Especially now that I completely understood how different Jag and I were and how I was the biggest loser to even think he would want me.

I'd been fine with the way things were between us. I'd even had some dignity about the whole thing. Now, though? I felt like an idiot and a fool—a whore with no common sense at all.

Jag was too good to be true, is what it was. Anyone could be that amazing for a small amount of time. But his assistant probably knew him better than anyone else did. She quickly pointed out how much better he was than me and how he'd already stopped thinking about me and how he was preparing to take off on his next quest.

The way my mind whirled inside my head made me feel sick to my stomach. I'd taken a walk around town to try and make the feeling go away.

"Hey, Millie," a man said, making me spin around with hope that Jag had come looking for me.

"Oh, it's just you, Sammy." Sammy was five years older than me. He'd been after me since I was in my junior year of high school. And I'd never liked that about him. I hadn't wanted to talk to him then, and I still felt the same way now. "I'm kind of busy."

"Sure you are." He stepped in beside me. "So, I caught the show last night. Who's the new guy?"

"Nobody." I wasn't going to tell him a thing about Jag.

"So, I guess he didn't tell you that he's going to invest in the brewery. Probably because he was too busy sticking his tongue down your throat." He laughed at his sick joke.

"I'm aware of why he's in town, Sammy. And what I do is really none of your business, or anyone else's for that matter." I picked up my pace. I didn't want to be near the man.

"Who knows, he might even move here."

"Who knows?" I gained speed, putting space between us.

"Think he's gonna still be interested in you if he ever comes back?"

"Who knows? See ya." I turned the corner to get away from him.

Sammy's words began seeping into my addled brain. *If he ever comes back?*

He hadn't left yet. Not that I knew of. There was still a slight chance that he'd come and see me before leaving. Even though I had said all the things that I'd said.

Changing directions, I headed back toward Main Street, so I could see whether Jag's enormous RV was still in the park. The closer I got, the faster I went, until I was running.

Going around the corner, I jumped up on the sidewalk that ran along Main Street, searching for the RV that should've been in the distance. But it wasn't there.

Running faster, I went out into the road. *Nothing.*

Standing there, I couldn't believe it. *He left without saying goodbye.*

His assistant hadn't lied to me. She hadn't been just trying to get me to leave Jag alone at all. She'd been extremely honest with me.

Once Jag walked away from me, his mind went right on to the next thing. And I didn't know why my heart hurt so badly just from finding out that I'd been told the truth.

I should've known someone like Jag would have one of those minds that just keeps moving. He was super rich and still young. To get to where he was, he had to have been one of those fast movers and quick thinkers.

I was just a speed bump to him.

Nothing more than something that took up some of his time. Time that he mostly used to make money. But me and money had nothing in common.

His assistant was right about me. I wasn't in his league. I didn't have what it would take to keep Jag's attention for long. And I never would.

I can't believe he left without saying a damn thing to me.

The sound of a horn came from behind me and for a moment, I thought about not moving from the middle of the street. For the briefest of moments, I thought that I didn't really matter at all—and I never would.

"Millie!" I heard my sister's voice call out. "Wake up and get the heck out of the way before you get run over!"

Oh, yeah. I matter to my sister.

Shaking off the negative feelings I'd been having, I thought about the fact that I didn't just matter to my sister. She needed me. She relied on me for everything. And that was okay. That was how it was meant to be. At least, for a few more years. Like five or six of them.

"Why in the world were you standing in the road, looking at nothing at all?" she asked, stepping in beside me as I walked toward home. "It almost looked like you were about to start crying or something."

"I wasn't about to cry," I mumbled, feeling the sting of unshed tears as they burned the backs of my eyes.

"So, what were you doing out there like that?"

"Nothing." I didn't want to talk at all.

"So, about that big tip you got yesterday," she said, moving in front of me and then turning to walk backward so that she could face me.

"So what about it?"

Trying to act cute, she ducked her head and batted her long eyelashes. "Well, can we maybe do something fun with some of it?"

I knew my sister too well. Now that she knew about the extra money—which shouldn't really be considered extra since we never had enough to make ends meet as it was—she would annoy me about spending it in an irresponsible manner.

With a shrug, I let her know how things worked in our little, poor-ass world, "I'd already planned on spending it on something we'll both think is fun."

Clapping her hands, she smiled, dancing along the sidewalk backward, thinking I was finally going to be cool for once. "Yes! So, bowling is fun for both of us. At least, it used to be. And we could get the giant nachos there too. The way we used to when..." She went silent.

"When Mom and Dad were around to take us. Yes, I know that. But I had another killer idea, Myra."

"Better than bowling and nachos?" she asked, looking as if she couldn't think of anything better than that.

"Even better." I knew I was being an asshole but couldn't find it in me to care at all.

"Better than that?" Placing her hands on my shoulders, she stopped me. "What's going to be fun for both of us?"

"Get this," I said with excitement in my voice, "I'm going to use that money to pay the electric bill so that we can keep on living the good life, Myra."

"The electric bill?" she moaned, turning around and walking away from me. "I should've known that you would ruin it. You're never any fun at all, Millie."

"It takes money to have the kind of fun that you want to have."

"Hey!" she said, perking up. "I've got fifty bucks from babysitting last night. I can see if any of my friends have money, and then I'll have someone to go bowling with and we can split the cost of nachos."

"Why would you waste your money on that crap? I'm sure there are a lot of more important things that you could use that money for. Things like, oh I don't know, new shoes for school."

Her eyes just about popped out of her head. "I've got to buy my own shoes now?"

"Why not? If you're making some money, you should spend it on things that matter. Not junk. Not crap. Things you need, not merely want. You need some shoes. Now, you can buy some."

"What a bore you are, Millie. A really big boring person. No wonder..." She shut her mouth tightly, then turned and ran off.

She didn't have to finish her sentence. I knew what she was going to say. *No wonder that guy took off and left you without even saying goodbye.*

I didn't have money to do fun things. I didn't have time to do them either. I had to be the responsible one, or who knew what would become of us. Myra was just too young to understand that, though. And I had gotten okay with her being mad at me for being that way.

Head down, I walked home, trying not to think about anything. But it wasn't easy to quit thinking about Jag—and why he'd left without saying a word.

I did have his phone number, though. *But should I call?*

Shoving my hands into my pockets, I knew the answer to the question I'd asked myself. Of course I couldn't call him. I mean, I could call him because I had his number. But if I called him, it would cost me more than what I had to spare. It would cost me more dignity than I had already lost.

I had Jag's number. That much was true. But Jag knew where I lived. It wasn't like he didn't have any way of contacting me before he stepped into his big-ass RV and drove out of town.

It wasn't easy to take, but his assistant had been right. I just hadn't really wanted to believe it. And now that the truth had been shoved into my face, I had no choice.

I had to forget about him. That's all there was to it. I had to forget that Jag ever existed. I had to let go of the memories. I had to let it all go, or I would go crazy.

Like everything else, I didn't have time to go crazy. Going crazy was a luxury. Like so many other things that had become luxuries after my parents died.

Electricity—that was a necessity. Nachos—that was a luxury. Paying rent—that was a necessity. Bowling—that was a luxury.

Our parents had not been well off. They had been what I called lower middle class. On Fridays, my father got paid. So every Friday had been pizza night.

Dad's paychecks had gone to the groceries, gas for the car, school lunches, clothes, and shoes for all of us. So, technically, pizza on Friday nights was part of the grocery budget that he was in charge of.

My mother got paid only once a month. Her paycheck was meant to cover the bills. The big bills—rent, electricity, car payment, insurance for the car, health insurance, cable TV, and the internet. But even with all that, she always had at least a hundred dollars to spare so that we could go do something fun once each month.

I had not aced any of their skills yet. Of course, I was only one person bringing in one income that didn't even come close to what either of them had made. But I had cut the bills. I had stripped them down to the bare minimum. Cable and internet were not part of the package. Neither was a car or car insurance. Going out for groceries was a thing of the past. Like I said, I had stripped it down to the bare minimum. We bought food when we could afford some, and that was it.

Even though I had grown up with pretty much just enough money, there was something in me that just wouldn't take charity. I wouldn't even call it pride, because it wasn't that.

There were people out there who had so much less than what my sister and I had. There were people who couldn't work, no matter how much they wanted to. There were people who had so many children to take care of that they couldn't afford daycare to go to work.

There were some who would argue that if you didn't have enough money to have that many children, you probably shouldn't have had that many in the first place. What I knew from the people I had grown up with was that no one had a child based on whether they could afford to have one or not.

In a perfect world, things would go perfectly, but that's not where we lived. We lived in the kind of world that left kids all alone to fend for themselves. Or they could ask for help—help from the government.

If I had asked for help from the government to take care of my younger sister, they would have taken her from me. My sister was ten years old when our parents died. Had it not been for support from the people of our town, the authorities would have taken over.

So yeah—I was dull, boring, and uncool. But I had kept our family together. What was left of it anyway.

As I walked back home, something began to seep into my head. I had gone out the night before. I had danced with a gorgeous man. I'd had the best time of my life. During all that, my little sister had babysat a couple of unruly toddlers. And I was not without some way of rewarding her for what she had done.

It wasn't often that I used my resources—mostly because I didn't want to abuse my right to them. They weren't unlimited by any means. But not only did I owe it to my little sister, I also owed it to myself to splurge using some free resources.

Pulling my cell phone out of my pocket, I called the diner and placed an order for super supreme nachos. They weren't on the menu, and Freddie hated making things that weren't on the menu. So I had never asked him to make anything that wasn't on it. But he agreed to do it for me anyway.

A half hour later, Myra and I sat at the diner and we ate those free super supreme nachos with smiles on our faces. And we talked about the things we used to do before the wreck when Mom and Dad had been there with us.

As we sat in the corner booth, it became clear to me that I needed to spend more time with my sister. It became clear to me that I had to make time for other people as well as the one family member I had left. But it also became clear to me that I had missed one of the biggest opportunities of my life.

I'd missed the opportunity to be a friend—or maybe even more—to Jag. He'd lost as much as I had. But he'd chosen such a different route. Still, we had a lot in common, and I'd blown it all off—the way I always had.

Chapter Thirteen

Jag

A month had passed since my visit to Shiner. Not one day of that entire month did I not think about Millie. I had even searched for her on social media, hoping that she had changed her mind and opened an account. But so far, I hadn't seen hide or hair of her online.

The owners of the brewery had taken my offer, and production was supposed to have begun. So, I would have plenty of products to take to Germany with me when I went in a few months. I needed to check on the inventory at the brewery to make sure things were going the way they were supposed to be going, so I had good reason to make another visit to Shiner.

I had to admit to myself that when Millie didn't call, my ego had become quite bruised. It was that bruised ego that had kept me from going back to Shiner earlier. I would surely run into Millie and then I would have to inevitably ask why she hadn't called.

As I sat at my desk, gazing out the window of my Dallas home, something occurred to me that hadn't before. Maybe Millie was intimidated by my money. Maybe she hadn't called because she thought that I didn't really want anything else to do with her. But she couldn't have been more wrong.

I needed to do something different. I needed to stop waiting for her phone call. I needed to stop waiting to see if she would show up on social media. It was time for me to get proactive. So, that's exactly what I did.

"Miss Petty, can you come in here for a minute?"

She had been in her office, one room over from mine, doing something on the computer. But whatever business she was dealing with could wait. There was something much more important that I needed her to take care of.

"Yes, Jag, what can I help you with?" Smiling away as she walked into the room, she always seemed eager to help me with whatever I needed. I thought she had to be the best assistant anybody had ever had.

"I know you have your opinion about the girl from Shiner. But I'm going to ask you to do something for me, and I'm also going to ask you to please keep your opinion to yourself this time." I didn't need her trying to talk me out of doing something that I knew I wanted to do.

"If you need me to keep my opinions to myself, then I will keep my opinions to myself. What is it that you need me to do, Jag?"

Happy to hear that she wasn't going to argue with me about it, I said, "I want you to go back to Shiner. I want you to go to the diner on Main Street where Millie works. I want you to tell her that I am inviting her to come to Dallas this coming weekend. Let her know that her sister can come as well because I know she won't come without her."

She wore a troubled expression as she asked, "Am I to bring her back with me?"

"No. Tell her that I'll come and pick them up myself."

"I don't understand why you want me to go and ask her if she wants to spend the weekend with you here in Dallas if you're just going to pick her up yourself. What I'm saying is, why not ask her yourself?"

I hadn't really wanted to explain why I was reluctant to simply go to Millie—to see her face-to-face, in the flesh, and have her reject me. "I don't want to put any undue pressure on her to take my offer," I came up with. "I want her to come only if she wants to. And if I'm standing there waiting for an answer, then she might feel forced to tell me what I want to hear. So, that's why I'm asking you to do it. Will you?"

"I'm your assistant, Jag. It is my job to do the things you ask me to do. I did make a promise that I would keep my opinions to myself, but you should know that I think this is a terrible idea."

"You might be right. I mean, who really knows? But my gut is telling me that it's time to reach out to her."

"You gave her your phone number, remember?" she brought up. "Don't you think that if she wanted to see you or hear from you, she would have called you by now?"

"Of course I think that. But I think a lot of other things too. Things like she thinks I'm too busy to be bothered. Which I'm totally not. She might be thinking that I don't want anything else to do with her. She might be worried that I'll reject her the same way I'm worried she might reject me. Childish, I know, but it is what it is. So, I need a third party who has nothing to lose or gain and who can't be hurt with words of rejection. That's you, Miss Petty."

"So, you don't want me to talk her into coming? Is that right? If she says no right off the bat the way I think she probably will, then you want me to accept that no and just leave? Is that correct?"

I had to think about that one. I didn't know Millie all that well, but what I did know about her was that she was probably going to say no at first. So, I really didn't know what to tell Miss Petty. I decided to ask her a question instead, "Do you think you could feel her out? You know, try to sense if she's saying no just to say no? Maybe not put any pressure on her but give her a little time to change her mind or think about it? Say, maybe you tell her that I wanna see her for the weekend—that I'm inviting her up to Dallas, where she and her sister will have their own rooms."

"And then what?" she asked, crossing her arms over her chest.

"And then you tell her that you don't want her answer right away. Tell her you're gonna give her time to think about it. Then I want you to leave the diner and go to the brewery."

"And what am I to do at the brewery?"

"I want you to see how the production is going with the stock that I'm supposed to be taking to Germany in a few months."

"Okay, so I take some time finding out how production is going, and then you want me to go back to the diner and see if she has her answer ready. Right?"

"Yes, that's right."

"If she says no at that time, then I take her answer and leave? Is that what you want me to do?"

I still wasn't sure, so I asked her another question, "Do you think you would be able to tell if she's just saying no out of stubbornness? Because if she's just saying no to be stubborn, then of course I would want you to give her more time or maybe prompt her to come up with a reason why she's saying no. You know, like ask her if she can give you a reason so that you can let me know why she's refusing this generous offer. Or something like that."

"What happened to not putting any pressure on her to say yes? You must realize that if I start asking for reasons, that can put pressure on her. So, I need to know—do I put some pressure, do I put no pressure, do I put medium pressure?"

"How about a subtle amount of pressure? And make it as subtle as possible. Like, so under the wire that she won't even pick up that it's pressure. Think you can do that for me?"

"I can do that for you. You want her here for the weekend. Today is Monday. When would you like me to go? And before you say today, you should realize that she might say yes but change her mind by the end of the week."

I hadn't even thought about that. "I'm glad you're bringing this up. I hadn't even thought about it. But you're right. Maybe go on Wednesday because then she really won't have time to sit around and think about it and get spooked and then change her mind about coming."

"You should make an itinerary of what you would do with her and her sister during the weekend stay. Because she's sure to ask that. Any woman would want to know what you have planned."

"Man, something else I haven't thought about. What should I plan to do?"

"So, you want me to come up with an itinerary as well?" she asked, with a scowl on her face.

I began to feel as if I was asking too much of her. And since she didn't even think it was a good idea to invite Millie to spend the weekend with me, I couldn't even really trust her with taking on the task of finding things for us to do as entertainment. "No, I should do that."

"Okay, you have until Wednesday morning to get that all figured out. I'll call ahead to the brewery to set up the visit."

Filled with apprehension at the thought of Millie finding out that someone from my camp would be in Shiner on Wednesday, I asked, "What if someone tells her that we're coming?"

"I can't just show up at the brewery unannounced," she said with aggravation filling her voice. "It's unprofessional, Jag."

"Call on Wednesday morning while you're on the way down there. Tell them that I asked you to do an impromptu visit because you're on your way there to do something else."

"And if your precious Millie gets a heads up about that, then what?" she asked, brows raised as if she thought herself clever for coming up with the idea.

"You know that I can see right through you, right? You think this is a bad idea. You don't want me to have anything else to do with Millie. So you're coming up with anything that you think will make me just drop this whole plan."

"I am merely bringing up situations that may turn problematic. Perhaps we should just leave the brewery out of this. You should also think about this. If Millie thinks she's merely being invited to come and stay with you because I already happened to be in town on business, then she's going to think that you didn't send me there just for her."

"You're probably right about that."

"I am right about that. If you want to make her feel special, you won't add anything to my reasons for being in Shiner. Make this all about her and nothing else."

"You're right." I came up with another idea. "When I take them back, I can go and visit the brewery myself. Or I can visit it when I pick them up."

Pinching the bridge of her nose, she shook her head slowly before looking at me with an expression that told me I was clueless. "When I say leave the brewery out of it, I mean leave it out completely. Don't make a visit at all. Not when you go to pick her up. Not when you take her back. As a matter of fact, I wouldn't even mention the brewery or your business with it. Unless she asks. Make it about her, not about anything else."

She'd given me some excellent advice, and I would have been a fool not to take it. "Okay, I hear ya. No mention of the brewery, no mention of business of any kind. And now, I need to find some fun things for us to do."

"I'll let you get to work on that then. I've got things I'll need to wrap up since I'll be spending Wednesday traveling to get you a date for this weekend."

Sitting there alone after she left, I had to admit that I was being an enormous coward, sending my assistant to do what I should be doing for myself. Even though I normally gave off the vibe of being super confident, I was not that way on the inside.

Losing my mother and not having a father had left me sort of vulnerable, and not only did my ego bruise rather easily, but I also had a hard time dealing with rejection. I kept telling myself that no one likes to be rejected and that the way I felt was completely normal. But something inside of me told me that it wasn't as normal as I made it out to be.

"Miss Petty," I called out.

She walked back into the room, leaned on the doorframe, arms folded in front of her, and asked, "What can I do for you now, Jag?"

"Maybe don't go to Shiner. I'm going to come off like a coward if I send you."

Chewing on her lower lip, she seemed to be thinking about that for a moment. Then she looked at me and said, "Men of your financial status often send their assistants to do things for them. Most men like you are very busy and don't have time for most personal things. Maybe I can put on an air that says you would've come yourself had you not been so wrapped up in business dealings. And I could put a romantic spin on it—say that you're so busy because you wanted to free up the weekend so that you could spend all of it with your girl."

"See, I knew I hired the right person as my assistant. You can find the silver lining in everything."

"I do try." With a smile, she turned and left. "I will make you shine in that girl's eyes. You'll see. Leave it all to me."

For someone who didn't think Millie and I would ever work out, Miss Petty certainly was willing to go the extra mile to help me out with getting her into my life.

She probably thinks we'll crash and burn in spectacular fashion, and I'll learn my lesson. Hope she's not right about that.

Chapter Fourteen

Millie

Carrying a load of dirty dishes to the kitchen, I grumbled obscenities under my breath as my cell phone rang in the pocket of my jeans. The diner was packed with rude teenagers who'd rode in on a school bus from LaGrange to play baseball with the Shiner high school team. With hours to go on my shift, I was already tired and wanted nothing more than to go home and get off my aching feet.

My cell kept ringing as I put the dishes down in the sink then took it from my pocket, finding that it was my sister. Swiping the screen, I said, "What's so important that you're calling me during the lunch rush?"

"I came home to change my pants. Mother Nature snuck up on me today. You and I have been on the same monthly schedule for so long that I've gotten used to you making sure we had what we needed to tend to the bloody mess. But we're out."

"Yeah, I haven't bought any of that stuff since my last period."

"Well, wouldn't there still be some left if that was just last month?" she asked. "A new box usually lasts us a couple of months."

"Well, I didn't use the last one. I'm sure it was you who did."

"Yeah, I remember throwing the box away now that you brought it up. But how come you haven't bought more?"

"Because I haven't needed anything like that." I walked back out to tend to the noisy kids who couldn't stop asking for things, wearing a frown.

"You haven't needed them?" she asked. "Millie, think about what you've just said."

Time began to add up inside my brain, and I froze in place. "I'm late."

"You know, come to think of it, I never noticed any missing pads except the ones I used last month. You didn't have a period last month, and now you should be starting, but you're not. Do you know what this means?"

"Shit!" Untying my apron, I ran back to the office and tossed it on the desk before rushing out the back door. "I'll go buy some pads and drop them at the apartment for you so that you can get back to school."

"Millie?" she asked. "Are you going to get yourself a little something too?"

"I don't want to talk about it. I'll be there in a few minutes." Sprinting out of the diner, I slowed my pace only a little as I went to the dollar store just down the street.

Grabbing a box of pads off the shelf, I eased to the side to look at the pregnancy tests. Looking around, I made sure no one saw me as I picked one up then hurried to the checkout counter.

The old lady who'd worked there forever asked the same question she always did. "Will this be all for you?"

"Yes." My body shook as I waited for her to scan the pregnancy test, all the while praying that she didn't ask me anything about it.

Beep. Beep. She scanned the two items then placed them in a bag. "That'll be ten fifty-nine."

"It's not for me," I said as I placed the money on the counter.

"It's not my business," she replied, winking at me.

Blushing, I didn't even wait for my change as I took the bag and left. When I got to the apartment, I pulled the pregnancy test out of the bag then tossed it on the couch before running to the bathroom.

"Hey!" Myra shouted as she came out of her room. "Did you get the stuff?"

"On the couch." Closing the door behind me, I locked it. "Please, don't be positive."

Two minutes later I sat on the toilet, looking at the little stick with a plus sign on it. And then I threw up.

There wasn't time for me to cry. There wasn't time for me to completely break down. I had to get back to work. So I washed my face, rinsed my mouth with water, then walked out of the bathroom, trying not to look like my world was falling apart.

"You okay? I heard you throwing up?" Myra asked.

Nodding, I didn't think I could talk without crying. I kept heading for the door.

"You going back to work?"

I nodded again.

"Okay, I'll see you when I get home from school then."

With one more nod, I walked out of the door and went back to work, thinking that I would never forget the Wednesday when I took a test that changed my entire life.

Coming in through the front door of the diner, Rachel spotted me and headed my way. "Where did you go? We're swamped here, and you decided to just disappear?"

Gulping back the knot that had formed in my throat, I said quietly, "I had to do something for Myra. Sorry."

Moving past her, I went to put my apron back on before getting back to work. I felt numb. I couldn't think straight at all.

"Miss, can I have more water?" one of the teens asked me.

"You want water?" I asked, noticing that my voice sounded distant.

"Yes. Are you okay? You're like super pale right now."

"I'll get your water," I said without responding to his question.

Filling a pitcher with ice, I turned the faucet on to put water into it, then went back to the table, filling the empty glass. "Thanks," he said.

"No problem," I said, wondering what the hell I was going to do.

Someone came into the diner, and I looked at the door to see who it was. Blinking a few times, I couldn't believe what I saw. "No way."

She held her hand up, gesturing for me to come to her. "Millie, can you spare a moment?"

What the hell is Jag's assistant doing here?

Some relief began to fill me as I went to her. There was no way I could handle having a baby all on my own. I had to tell Jag about the pregnancy. "Samantha, right?" I asked to make sure.

"Yes. Can we talk, or are you too busy?"

"I really need to talk to you." Looking over my shoulder, I saw Rachel hustling as fast as she could to deal with all the customers. "We're a waitress short today. Follow me. I'll get you seated and be with you as soon as these people thin out a bit. Want something to drink?"

"Sure. Anything will be fine." She took a seat at the small table I led her to. "There's no rush at all."

I left her and went to get her a glass of sweet iced tea, my body tingling as I hoped Jag would be coming in soon too. Going back to her table, I put the glass in front of her. "So, is Jag not too far behind you?"

"He's not in town."

I deflated instantly. "Oh."

"Miss, I need some more ketchup over here," one of the teens called out.

"I'll be back as soon as I can." I turned my attention to the customers. I had a mission to get them done and out, so I could figure out why Jag's assistant was in town, sitting in the diner, waiting to talk to me.

While working, I went over the last conversation she and I had.

"Can I help you?"

"I'm Millie. Is Jag here?"

"No. So you are the one he spent the night with."

"He told you about that?"

"Yes. Jag and I are very close. He tells me everything."

"I'm sorry. He hasn't told me anything about you. You are?"

"I am Samantha Petty, his assistant. And he's told me everything about you, Millie Powers."

"Does he talk to you about all the girls he's interested in?"

"Let's not go there. See, the thing is that you aren't in his league. You know that, though. You did the right thing when you told him that it's best for you two to part ways without trying to stay connected by anything."

"I know he's got money and I've got very little. But I'm not really out of his league. He and I have a lot in common. Did he tell you that?"

"That doesn't matter at all. You are never leaving this town, and Jag's future is in world travel. You would be out of your comfort zone, to say the least."

"I can't travel anywhere while I'm still taking care of my sister."

"That's what I'm saying. You can't be what he needs. You've got your things to do, and he's got his. Your worlds collided only briefly. Be happy with what you got from him but don't expect anything more. If not for his sake, then for your own. You don't know him the way I do. He's sure to break your heart. It sounds like your heart isn't in the best of shape after losing your parents. If I were you, I wouldn't test it."

"Why are you so sure he would break my heart?"

"I've known him for many years. I've seen him in action. He's never stayed in a relationship for more than a month or two. His mind moves fast. He's into one thing and then on to another before you know it. It's just who he is. We're leaving here today. He's set up a meeting in San Antonio for tonight. If he was as into you as you think he is, then why would he want to leave this town so quickly?"

"I see. Well, I wish him well. Can you tell him that for me?"

"Honestly, it's best if you don't think about him anymore. Enjoy your memories. But don't think anything more will come of that one night. His mind is already moving on, and it hasn't been but a few hours since you two parted company. Best you do that too, dear."

She'd been wrong about nothing coming from that one night. And once most of the customers had cleared out, I took her to the office, closed the door, then got right to it. "It's kind of amazing that you're here today of all days."

"Why is that?" she asked, as she sat in the chair in front of the desk.

"I found out something just a little while ago. And Jag needs to know about it. But first, why did you come to see me?"

Shaking her head, she said, "You tell me what Jag needs to know first, and we'll go from there."

I thought it best to say it straight out. "I'm pregnant. I've been in a trance since I found out. I can't do this alone. I hadn't thought that far ahead, but I'm going to call Jag to tell him once I'm done with my shift."

"No," she said calmly. "That's not a good idea at all."

"He has to know that he's going to be a father. And I can't do this on my own." There was no way I wasn't going to tell Jag about this baby. "He's all alone in the world with the death of his mother. This will be the only blood he shares with anyone. It's his right to know about the baby."

She looked at me with a cynical stare. "Are you prepared to deal with the consequences of telling him about this baby? Because there will be many consequences, Millie."

"I don't understand." I didn't expect her to be happy about the news—she'd been blunt with me about how she thought we were in different leagues. But there was a baby now that would connect Jag and I for the rest of our lives.

"Let me just say this," she said. "How can we be sure that baby is his?"

"I haven't been with anyone but him in the last few years, so I know it's his."

"How can I know that you're telling me the truth?"

"I guess you can't know that I'm telling the truth. It's not like I would deny Jag the right to have a paternity test. If he wants one, he can get one once the baby is born. But he should get to be there for all of this. If you think that I believe that this means he and I will be together, I don't. But we can raise this child together. It's his right, Samantha."

"You have no idea what you would be getting into if you told him about this. No idea at all. You don't know that man the way I do."

"I know he's the father of this baby, and I know that I'm going to tell him about it, whether you like it or not. This really has nothing to do with you."

"You're right. It doesn't. It's just that, as a woman, I feel the need to look out for you. You seem strong in a way, but you also seem very weak in others. I don't think you have the strength to go up against him."

"Why would I need to go up against Jag? I'm not trying to fight with him over this, I just want to share our child. I want nothing more than that. I'm not some gold digger. I didn't do this on purpose. I think Jag will understand that. I think he'll want to know about the pregnancy, and I think he'll want to be a part of his child's life."

"He will. You are right about that. He won't turn his back on a child that's his. You should understand that about him," she said with a grim expression that didn't quite match the words coming out of her mouth. "He will share blood with this baby. This will be the only person on Earth he will share that with. And that will be huge for him."

"I agree. I must admit that I wasn't sure what I thought about this baby. I'm still pretty numb from the shock of it all. But I want this baby. And I'm sure Jag will want it too."

"I agree."

"So, I don't see the problem."

"I can see that you don't." She stood, facing me, then put her hands on my shoulders. "I'm going to educate you on Jag Briggs, Millie. You need to know a lot more about him before you go telling him something like this."

"Wait a minute. You came here for some reason. What was it?"

"He wants you to come to Dallas to spend this weekend with him. But you're not going to take his offer."

"And why wouldn't I?" Spending the weekend with him sounded like the perfect thing to do, since we had a lot to discuss about our baby.

"Take a seat, and I will tell you why that is."

Damn, this sounds bad.

Chapter Fifteen

Jag

I'd been on pins and needles all day. I'd expected a call by now. With no word of Millie's answer, I feared the worst. Sending Miss Petty to do what I should've done myself might have been a giant mistake.

When my cell rang, I exhaled, feeling a little relaxation come over me with Miss Petty's call. "Hey, what did she say?"

"Nothing," she said. "She's left town. And no one knows where she went."

"No way." That was impossible to believe. "Are you screwing with me?"

"I would never do that, and you know it. She's moved away."

"She wouldn't do that. She's got no one. The people in that town are her family. She wouldn't leave them. What about her sister?"

"They're both gone. From what Millie's coworkers told me, Millie left a note on the door of the diner, saying that she and her sister were moving away and wouldn't be coming back."

"There is no way that Millie did that." I began to think that Millie just didn't want to see me and had come up with an elaborate ruse to try to fool me into thinking that she was gone. "They must be lying to you. I need you to go to her apartment. I can see her friends and coworkers lying to you about her whereabouts, but I doubt her landlord would lie to you."

"If she's gone to these lengths to avoid you, then why would you even want anything to do with her?" she asked, sounding confused.

"I'm not sure I would want anything to do with her if she's capable of doing something like this. But I can't believe she would move away. And I can't believe she wouldn't have told anyone where she was going. I can't believe any of this. But, if she's really gone, that worries the shit out of me."

"She's a grown woman, Jag. I don't think there's a need to worry about her."

"This isn't like her." I knew she would never just leave town that way.

"Jag, you don't really know her. You can't make a judgment call like that when you've only spent a handful of hours with her. I'm sorry. I know you're disappointed. But you'll be fine."

"Not until I know she's okay."

"I'm sure that if she had any problems, she would have contacted someone. Whatever her reason for leaving, we'll never know. Mostly because it's none of our business."

"What if she didn't leave on her own? What if someone forced her to leave? What if she and her sister were kidnapped and something terrible has happened to them?"

"Nothing like that happened. She simply found somewhere else where she wanted to live and moved there."

"Why would she not tell anyone where she was moving to then?" Nothing was making any sense.

"I don't know. Nor does anyone I've talked to about her. Her friend, Rachel, speculated that she might have run off with an old boyfriend. She said that Millie might not have wanted anyone to know about her going back to one of her old flames, which is a possible explanation for why she left in secret."

"I can't see her doing that to her sister."

"That's only because you don't really know her, Jag. I'm on the way back now. I hope you can put her out of your mind. She's gone, and it's highly doubtful you'll ever cross paths again."

"You don't know that. You don't even know where she is. For all we know, she might be right here in Dallas."

"Or Canada," she said. "We might not ever know where she is."

"She must have enrolled her sister in school. I wonder if there's some national registry that tells you which school a person is attending?"

"There's not. I think schools have rules about things like that. It would violate the student's privacy if they put that information out for anyone to get."

She was probably right. But there had to be a way to track Millie down. "Hey, what about her boss? If she's gotten a job wherever she is, then he might've been called as a reference. Did you talk to him?"

"He wasn't there."

"I'll call the diner."

"Jag, stop it. Millie has moved on. You should too. And what if your instincts are right, and she's just told her friends to say that she's moved? You're going to feel terrible if that's the case. Let it go."

"I just can't. What if something has happened to her?"

"If something has happened to her, how would you find out anyway?"

"Did you ask if anyone tried to find her?" It would be crazy if no one was worried about her unexpectedly leaving her hometown. "I'm sure lots of people there have her cell phone number. Has anyone tried calling her or her sister to see where the hell they went?"

"I'm sure they did do that. But apparently, neither Millie nor her sister answered any of their calls."

"Well, that's highly suspicious. Maybe I should put in a call to the police in Shiner. Maybe they should be looking into this."

"Jag, would you listen to yourself? You sound like a crazy person. I'm sure the police have better things to do than trying to find someone who has simply relocated."

"Where did she get the money to move? She doesn't even own a car. Did she walk away?"

"You're not thinking rationally. It's obvious that someone came and picked her up. Like her friend said, probably some old boyfriend. It wouldn't be the first time something like that happened."

"Yeah, but this isn't like Millie. She's an honest person."

"Again, how would you know that? You don't really know her. For all you know, she's a humongous liar."

She was right—I didn't know Millie well enough to say anything about her. "It's just that this is really confusing, and I can't help but be worried about her."

"I know you're worried. But I honestly don't think you have any reason for that. No one else seems worried about her. I would think that the people she's known her whole life would worry if it were warranted."

"You're probably right about that." It seemed to me that if no one was worried about Millie, they knew she hadn't moved away at all and were just saying that because Millie didn't want anything to do with me.

"I am right about that."

"Okay, I tried anyway. That's all I can do."

"That is all you can do. Just let it go, Jag. She has."

That was obvious. Whether she'd left town with an old boyfriend or just had everyone lying to keep me away from her, Millie had let me go for good.

I didn't even know why I felt such disappointment. I replayed our last conversation in my mind, searching for any hope in the words she'd said to me.

"You know, this doesn't have to be a one-time thing."

"Let's not go there, Jag. I like that we're parting on good terms. No bad feelings between us. You know?"

"Yes, I get it. But that doesn't mean that we can't stay in touch and see each other every now and then."

"It won't be easy. I'm not one to sit and talk on the phone. And my schedule is chaotic, to say the least. I work as much as they'll let me. And when I'm not working, I'm helping my sister with homework, doing laundry, or cleaning the apartment. There's always something that needs to be done."

"Okay, I won't bring it up anymore. If we meet again, then we meet again. If that's how you want it."

"Yes, that is exactly how I want it."

"So, you're not going to give me your number, is what you're saying."

"That's right."

"Do you still have mine? Or did you throw it away?"

"I've got it. I'm not going to use it, though. So, don't go waiting for a call to come. I'm probably going to toss it anyway. Just to be sure that I don't get all into my feelings and call you sometime."

"But you can if you want to. I'm not nearly as busy as you are. I'm free to talk whenever you want. Don't toss my number, is what I'm trying to say here."

"I don't know. I'll think about it. I'm not promising anything, though."

"Yeah, I can see that you don't like to make promises, Millie."

"Oh, I make plenty of them, Jag. I promised to take care of my sister, and that's my number one priority. I think you can make it back to the RV park from here, Jag."

"It's pretty dead here this morning."

"It'll liven up around noon. Are you planning on letting my hand go?"

"So, this is it then? No breakfast together?"

"No. Thank you for asking, though. You're a nice guy, Jag. I'm glad we got to know each other. You won't be forgotten."

"Neither will you. How about lunch? I'll take you and your sister to lunch. Anywhere you want."

"You've got the brewery thing to do. Do what you came here to do. Don't let me get in your way. I wasn't the reason why you came here. Remember that you have a goal here, and I wasn't any part of that. Stay the course, Jag."

"Jag Briggs. Remember my whole name just in case you ever want to look me up on social media or anything. I've got homes in Dallas, Los Angeles, and New York. My social media profile says that Los Angeles is where I'm from, though. You can instant message me if you ever lose my number. So, what about your social media info?"

"I'm not on it. There's no time for anything like that."

"No way, Millie. Everyone is on some type of social media platform. Don't try to bullshit me."

"Not me, Jag. Let's not make this awkward or weird or anything that will take away from the night we had. So, see you if I see you, Jag Briggs."

"Millie?"

"Yes."

"What's your last name? Just in case you do ever get on social media."

"Powers."

"Okay. If you ever do get on social media and I send you a friend request, you had better accept it."

"I won't—but okay."

"Promise?"

"I promise. And I don't break promises. But don't go holding your breath. I don't have time for things like that. Thank you."

"Just so you know, I'm only letting you go because I respect the shit out of you."

"Thank you. I respect you too. Keep doing you, Jag. It's worked great so far. And I'm sure it always will."

"Yeah, so far it's worked out for me. And you make sure you take your turn when the time comes. Promise me—one day you will do you, Millie Powers. I know you'll be great at whatever you decide to do."

"I promise you. One day, when it's my turn, I will do me, Jag. And thanks for believing in me. That means a lot. It really does. I've got to go."

"Okay. See you, Millie."

"Yeah, see ya, Jag."

Millie hadn't wanted any bad feelings between us. She didn't want to ever tarnish the memories of our one night together. So I had to admit to myself that she just didn't want to see me again.

Getting everyone to say she'd moved away was a bit much, though. She didn't have to go that far. She could have just told Miss Petty that she wasn't interested in seeing me again. It wasn't like I wouldn't take no for an answer.

But what if she really did move?

What if something had happened to her? What if everyone she knew thought that she'd just run off with a guy, and she didn't want anyone to know about it? But what if she hadn't done that?

I knew I should've just left it alone. There was a high chance of her rejecting me once I did find her. But I had to find her anyway. I had to know if she was okay.

If she didn't want anything to do with me, then that would be fine. But I still had to make sure that nothing bad had happened to her. I couldn't not care. I couldn't not worry. And I wasn't about to try to make myself do those things.

I could handle rejection. I could handle her being mad at me for finding her—if that was the case. What I couldn't handle was not having a clue if she was safe or not.

It was obvious that Miss Petty wasn't going to help me find Millie. And if I told her what I was going to do, she would bug the shit out of me to stop looking for someone who didn't want me to find them.

But what if Miss Petty was wrong about that? What if Millie had everyone say that she'd moved only to see to what lengths I would go to find her and make sure she was okay?

I could see a woman testing a man by doing something along those lines. Would I move heaven and earth for her? Would I go to the ends of the earth to find her?

Those are the sorts of things romance novels are made of. A love that knows no bounds. A love that will last a lifetime and then some. A love that will never fade away.

Love was a bit much to be talking about for two people who'd spent one hit night together. So, I wasn't about to go around even thinking that I was in love with Millie. But I was worried.

So, whatever this feeling was, it was one that wouldn't just go away. I couldn't simply let it go. Millie was missing as far as I knew.

Maybe she'd manufactured a lie, maybe she hadn't. Either way, I had to get to the truth. Even if it would hurt me in the end. I had to know the truth.

If Mille wanted a man who would walk through fire for her, then she just might get it. Because I was determined to find her. I was determined to get the truth out of her.

Hate me. Love me. Whatever. I had to know.

But I would most definitely have to keep what I was doing from Miss Petty. And that wasn't going to be easy since she was my assistant and had her hand in pretty much everything I did.

Time to come up with a plan to keep Miss Petty busy so that she won't know what I'm up to.

Chapter Sixteen

Millie

"But I can't leave everyone I've ever known behind without saying a word about where we're going or why we're suddenly moving away from the only town we've ever lived in," Myra complained as I shoved our clothes in trash bags.

"You know, you could do something to help instead of crying over this. I know this is bad. Or at least, it seems that way right now. But we're going to live in a beautiful house, drive expensive cars, and live a life we never could have dreamt of." If things hadn't been so rushed and we'd had enough time for this to sink in, we might've even been happy about the big changes we were about to make. "You're going to get to go to college, Myra. It'll be paid for. You won't have to borrow a dime in student loans. You won't have to start your adult life drowning in debt."

"I know that part is great. Most of it is pretty great. But leaving without telling anyone is really making me feel terrible. My friends are going to worry about me, Millie. And yours will too."

"I'm leaving the note that Samantha wrote. I'll tape it to the diner door right before we leave town tonight. After it's closed and no one will be around to see us leaving. We can't answer any questions about where we're going. Or he could find out. And we can't have that."

"She really thinks he'll try to take the baby?" she asked with a frown.

"She does. And she knows him much better than I do. I've got to trust her on this. It's too important not to. I can't lose this baby. I know it wasn't planned, but I don't want to have to give it away to him. I would love to share our child. But she's sure that he'll hire lawyers to get the baby—maybe even right after I give birth. That scares the hell out of me, Myra."

"Well, yeah. That sounds very scary. But how are you so sure that he would do that to you?"

"I'm not sure. Not a hundred percent anyway. But his assistant has known him since he was a kid, like eleven or so. She knows him, Myra, and I really don't. I just know the man he showed himself to be. But she said that he's the kind of person who puts on a good face, but then once he gets to you—especially to women—he becomes completely selfish. And he takes whatever he wants."

"But what if he won't do that to you, Millie?"

"I'm not about to risk losing my baby to find that out. Believe me when I say that I would so much rather not do this. My first instinct was to tell Jag about everything. I guess I'm very lucky that he sent his assistant today to ask me to go to his place in Dallas for the coming weekend. Otherwise, I would've made a huge mistake. She's really a godsend, is what she is. Giving me a home in Miami, and sending money each month for you and I to live on so that we won't have to get jobs. She said there are two cars in the attached garage too. It's got a pool and the house is like six thousand square feet. We're going to be set for life."

"But why would she do that, Millie?" Myra asked, sounding uncertain. "What does she have to gain from putting you and me and this coming baby into a home, giving us money to live on, cars to drive, money for college? It doesn't add up. I think you should slow down and think about this before we go all the way to Florida."

"There's no time. She's already called a car that will be here to pick us up at ten tonight. The driver will drive us all the way to the house in Miami. She's already told me where to find the car keys and the security code to get into the house. That's all we'll need to get inside."

"Why not fly us there if she's so rich?" Myra asked with a huff.

"She said that Jag would probably find out that she bought our tickets, and then he would know where we are. He did send her to me, you know. He wanted me to spend the weekend with him. So, he would most definitely want to look for us. She even texted me a little while ago that he had said something about coming to look for me and that he'd come up with several ideas of how to go about doing that. Things that would be an invasion of your privacy, Myra."

"My privacy?" she asked with wide eyes, finally beginning to understand the type of person I was dealing with.

"Yes, your privacy. He thought about asking your school some questions. Samantha told him that giving out information about students is against school policy or something like that. So, you can see that he's going to stoop to whatever level he has to."

Shivering, she wrapped her arms around herself. "Well, that's creepy."

I didn't want to think of Jag as creepy at all. The man I'd spent one amazing night with hadn't been that way. But how could I not take Samantha's warning to heart?

"Look, I just want to get the hell out of here. Once we're safe in Miami, then I can take some time to really think about Jag and this situation. The most important thing right now is to keep my baby safe. Tell me that you can understand that, Myra. Tell me that you won't go and call one of your friends, or anyone else, to tell them where we're going. Please, promise me that you won't do that."

"He doesn't know anything about me. He doesn't know any of my friends. So, you're worrying about nothing at all. If Elaina doesn't hear from me, she's gonna freak out. We've been best friends since kindergarten. We don't do anything without the other knowing about it."

She had a point. But telling anyone anything was much too dangerous. "Here's the reason you can't tell anyone—not even your best friend. See, you could tell Elaina, and you could even make her promise not to tell anyone about this. And for a while, she might be able to hold on to that secret. But the thing is that people will be talking about how we just up and left without saying a word to anyone. And then Elaina might tell someone who she thinks is very upset about our disappearing. She'll do it with the best of intentions too. But that person will feel like they have to tell another upset person, and that will continue until the whole damn town knows our secrets."

"Why not go to the police and tell them what Jag's assistant told you? Why not ask them for help?"

"What can they do? It's not exactly a crime for a man to take the mother of his baby to court to gain custody. The cops can't protect me from Jag's lawyers, Myra."

She finally grabbed a trash bag and headed to the bathroom. "I'll get our bathroom stuff."

"Glad to have you on the same page, sis."

"Oh, I'm not completely on the page you're on, Millie. But I'm not going to leave my things behind. I just hope that once we're settled into this new place, you'll come to the conclusion that Jag's assistant might not be telling you the truth about him. I just have this gut feeling that she's coming between you two for some reason. Maybe she wants him."

"She's old enough to be his mother, Myra," I said, shaking my head. I knew Samantha wasn't doing all this just to keep me and Jag apart. "Don't you remember me telling you that she's known him since he was around eleven years old? What kind of freak would she be if she liked him that way?"

"They make all kinds of freaks, Millie," she called out from the bathroom. "Should I take the soap too?"

I had no idea what Samantha had at the house. "Wrap it in toilet paper before you put it into the bag with the rest of the stuff."

Peeking around the corner, she asked, "Millie, how much money did that lady give you?"

I hadn't counted it, so I took the folded bills out of my front pocket. "I'm not sure. She handed me this and told me that it should get us through until she could figure out a way to get money to me without Jag ever finding out. I wasn't going to count it in front of her. That would've been super rude."

Coming to stand next to me, Myra looked at the cash in my hand. "That's a pretty thick stack of bills, Millie."

Unfolding the money, I found the first bill was a hundred. "If this is full of these, then we've got a heck of a lot of money."

"Count them," she said eagerly.

Each bill I folded down to count the next revealed another one that was just like the first one. All hundreds. I could not believe what I held in my hand. "There's thirty of them, Myra. I'm holding three-thousand dollars." My knees went weak, and I had to sit down, breathing heavily.

"Oh yeah!" Myra shouted as she pranced around the living room. "I'm getting waffles for breakfast in the morning! And we're gonna eat out every night!"

"Myra, we don't know how long it will be until Samantha figures out how to send us more money."

Stopping mid-dance move, her mouth hung open. "You're not going to spend the money?"

"Yes, I'll spend it. But I'll do it responsibly. We have to make this last."

"You suck, Millie Powers. You totally suck. You're sitting there with more money than you've ever had in your entire life, and all you can think about is spending it responsibly. God! I just want to live a freaking normal life for once. Do the things other people do. Things like eating out. Things like buying clothes from a real department store instead of the dollar store. Normal things!"

"Hey, brat," I said to stop her pity party. "All that's about to happen for us. Miami is where our normal life will begin. We'll live in a real house with really nice things in it. We'll drive nice cars. We'll be able to shop in the downtown stores of Miami, Florida. Like the rich people do. So, stop whining about how we've lived so far and start dreaming about a bright future."

"Fine," she said with a huff. "But can I please have waffles for breakfast? We're going to be riding in a car for hours upon hours to get to Miami. At least you can buy some food along the way."

She was right. I would probably need to buy us food along the way. "Fine. But you had better not try to order the expensive stuff off any menu. Look at the specials first, and that's what we'll order."

"Cheap-ass," she said, then got up and went back to the bathroom to finish packing. "I'm glad I can go to college. I'm going to get the best degree possible so that I can make the most money anyone has ever made."

"Good. I want you to do that."

"And when you come to me, asking for a handout, I'll give you five bucks, and that's it."

"How mean." Tying up the trash bag full of our clothes, I went to put it by the door.

"Yeah, I learned it from you, cheap-ass."

"No need to call me names, butt-head."

She carried the trash bag filled with our toiletries and put it next to the door. "How long before our ride arrives?"

"A couple of hours from now."

She looked around before taking a seat on the couch. "We don't have anything else to pack."

"It's kind of sad that all our things fit into a couple of trash bags." Looking at the bags by the door, I began to feel bad about the way I had us living all these years. "Mom and Dad wouldn't be proud of me." I sat down beside my sister. "I'm sorry that I haven't been a good provider for you, Myra."

Slipping her arm around my shoulders, she put her head on my shoulder. "They're very proud of you, Millie. You've done the best you could. You know something?"

"What?"

"You should totally go to college too. Even if that lady won't pay for yours the way that she said she'll do for me. That way, you can get a great job someday too."

"That's something to think about." With so much turmoil going on in my life at the time, I knew it wasn't the right time to be trying to concentrate on school. "My mind is sort of a mess right now. I can't wrap my head around much at all."

Lifting her head off my shoulder, she smiled at me. "Well, you might want to wrap your head around this. You're going to be a mother, Millie."

I hadn't even had time to think about that. "A mother. Me." Shaking my head, I couldn't even believe it. "It seems unreal to me."

"Well, it's real. You're going to have a little baby. I can't wait to hold it. I hope it's a boy." She laughed. "No, a girl." With a shrug, she said, "Whatever it is, I'll love it so much."

"I'm glad you're happy about becoming an aunt."

"I'm going to be the best aunt there's ever been. This baby is going to have so much love. I'm not happy about all this craziness, but I'm happy about the baby. Even if it has a dad who's a real meanie."

"You know, it's really hard for me to think of Jag that way. I mean, he came off sort of arrogant and bossy when I first met him, but then his demeanor changed, and there didn't seem to be a single bad thing about him. As a matter of fact, he seemed to be sort of fragile. You know, I wonder why he sent his assistant to ask me to go and spend the weekend with him instead of coming to ask me himself."

"Probably afraid of you rejecting him," she said.

"Yeah. See what I'm saying? He's sort of fragile. It's hard to believe he would do the things that Samantha is certain he'll do. Why would he want our baby all to himself if I am more than willing to share him or her? And we could do that any way he wanted to, as far as I'm concerned. Be together, don't be together, but parent our child *together*. Why wouldn't he want to work with me on this?"

"Selfish people don't like to work with others," she pointed out. "So, if he is the way that lady said he is, then I think you're right not to risk our baby."

Laughing, I asked, "*Our* baby?"

"Yeah, I'm taking some ownership of my niece or nephew because I'm going to be just as much in their life as you will. Aunt of the year. No. Aunt of the century!"

At least I've got my sister—I won't be all alone.

Chapter Seventeen

Jag

Two months went by without me finding hide or hair of the missing Millie. I had to admit I felt defeated. I'd come to realize that I relied on Miss Petty far too much.

Without being able to ask her for her help, I was getting nowhere. But I knew I couldn't ask her to do anything that had to do with Millie. So, I had to figure out something else.

I thought about hiring another assistant. Maybe a male—someone who could better understand why I needed to find Millie.

When a man can't let a day go by without thinking of a woman, it means there's something to it. It means the woman that he can't stop thinking of is much more to him than just some passing fascination. Millie was more than that to me. I couldn't stop thinking about her.

"What's this, Jag?" Miss Petty asked as she came outside where I was lying by the pool. She waved the piece of paper in her hand. Her eyes were narrow and her jaw was set—lips forming a thin line. It was clear that she was angry. "I happened to find this little note you jotted down to remind yourself that you are looking for another assistant. What could you possibly need that I don't already do for you?"

Busted!

Like a deer in the headlights, I stared at her, unsure of what to say and completely certain that I had screwed myself by writing down my thoughts. But then I remembered the paper had been on the desk in my office, and there was no reason for her to be in there. "What were you doing in my office?"

Without even blinking an eye, she said, "I was looking for something." She shook the paper in her hand again. "Now, tell me about you needing this new assistant."

"I just need one, is all."

"To do what?"

"Things."

"Don't try to be cute with me, Jag. Just be honest. Tell me why you need a new assistant. And is this assistant going to replace me, eventually? Because let me tell you, it isn't easy to work for you."

"You think I'm hard to work for?"

"Extremely."

"If I'm so hard to work for, how come you stuck around for so long?" I had no idea that she had not been happy being my assistant. But now that I knew that about her, I felt it might be time to let her move on to where she would be happy. "You're free to leave my employment anytime you want, Miss Petty."

"I'm not the one who's looking for a new assistant. I'm not the one keeping secrets. I don't want to leave this job. And I don't want to deal with this new person that you hire while I try to do the things you need me to do. So are you gonna tell me why you want to hire a new assistant?"

I couldn't tell her the truth. "I wasn't keeping a secret. You know how I'm going to Germany next week. I really can't take you with me because I need you here. So, I was thinking of hiring an assistant to accompany me there. Wasn't even sure if I was gonna keep him on after we come back."

"Why do you need me to stay here? I was planning on going with you to Germany."

"I need you to take care of things here. I've never told you that you were going to Germany with me, so why would you think that?" It was growing clearer and clearer that Miss Petty thought that she ran the show instead of me.

"I am your assistant, Jag. Naturally, I thought you would want me to go with you. I thought you would need me to go with you. You obviously need an assistant with you in Germany."

"And I also need someone here. There isn't time to train someone to do all the things that you do right here. And that's why I thought I would hire a new one. One who could come with me when I go out of the country to market whatever the heck I'm marketing at the time."

"If you're coming up with the idea of hiring a new assistant just now, then you don't have much time to find one. Getting me to help you do that would have been smart. I'm not even sure that one can be found in this short amount of time."

"I was thinking about hiring somebody fresh out of college. Just some guy. You know, a young guy who's ready to run at any time. Doesn't need a lot of time to pack. Someone who doesn't have any restrictions in life—a free spirit. I don't think that'll be that hard to find. And if they're fluent in several languages would be a plus. So, if you really want to help me, then put that out there wherever you put things for jobs and see what you can find for me. Unless you don't wanna help me do this. Because I can do it on my own. I don't need to have you doing every little thing for me."

"If you really don't need me to do every little thing for you, then why haven't you hired this new assistant already?"

She had a point, and I really didn't like that about her. "You know, maybe I've come to depend on you too much."

"No. You depend on me because you *should* depend on me. You pay me to assist you. And you pay me very well. So, I will go back inside, and I will get on the computer. I will go to the hiring website, and I will find you this young male assistant who is fluent in at least German and can leave the country as soon as next week."

"That would be great, thank you." Now that I had her working on that, I could focus on more important things. My plans for finding Millie.

This new assistant would have free time when we came back to the states. And during that free time, he could search for Millie. And Miss Petty would be none the wiser.

Only minutes had passed when she came walking back out to the pool, wearing a broad smile. "I've already hired your assistant."

"You've found my new assistant in twenty minutes?" I had a feeling this would be bad. "So when can he start?"

"He is my nephew. And he will be here tomorrow. I am flying him in from Sacramento tonight." She seemed to be thrilled with herself.

I wasn't thrilled at all with who she'd hired. "Your nephew speaks German?"

"And Chinese." She looked way too happy about it.

But I couldn't tell her nephew a thing about looking for Millie, or he would definitely tell his aunt. And that would not be good at all. "He has a passport?" I was looking for anything that would make it impossible for the guy to work out for me.

"Yes, he does. He's got it all, Jag. And best of all, he won't be a nuisance to me the way some stranger would." With a skip in her step, she turned and left.

Something didn't seem right about what she'd done. I had the feeling that she wanted someone with me who would tattle on me without any hesitation whatsoever.

Why would she want that?

I needed someone who I could trust, and she'd just eliminated that for me. What was worse was that I'd let her do it. I felt manipulated. And that didn't feel good at all.

Getting out of the pool, I walked into the house, using a towel to dry off as I went. "Hey," I shouted when I saw her coming out of her office. "Tell your nephew he's not needed. I've thought about it, and I don't really need anyone to go with me to Germany. That's precisely the reason I hadn't moved forward with hiring another assistant. I wasn't sure about it yet. And then you went and forced the issue, and I had to really think about it. Now, I have come to the conclusion that I don't even want anyone to go with me when I go do these marketing tours."

"No, it's a good idea for someone to go with you. It's not safe for you to go to other countries all alone. He's excited about it anyway. I can't disappoint him."

"Well, you're going to have to disappoint him because I'm not taking him with me. I am not hiring him, Miss Petty."

"You're acting strange," she told me.

"I'm just not cool with you taking over so much."

"I have always been the take-charge type, but you've never disliked that about me before. Why now?"

"I'm just not happy with you thinking that you can overrule me or are in charge of me in any way." I had to stop letting her get away with everything. "If you were anyone else, I wouldn't have let you have this much authority."

"You've given me all the authority that I have, Jag. You did it for a good reason. You need my help. Let Sean go with you to Germany and just see if the two of you mesh. If you don't like him for some reason, I'll tell him that you've changed your mind about needing an assistant to go with you on those tours. But give the kid a chance. Please. For me."

I wasn't sure what to do. I'd handled everything so wrong. "Look, this whole thing is my fault. And I am sorry for the misunderstanding. But I will not hire him. Frankly, I don't like the idea that you want your relative to accompany me. I feel like you want him around to spy on me and relay the information back to you."

"Well, that's just silly, Jag. I don't need anyone to spy on you. You're being foolish. Give him a chance."

"I said no." I couldn't let her win. I had to start a new narrative between us. "Miss Petty, I need to be more self-sufficient. You're actually *too* good at taking care of things for me. I've become dependent on you, is what I'm trying to say."

"Isn't that a good thing?" she asked, with arms akimbo. "You pay me well, Jag. I've been with you for many years. Shouldn't you be able to depend on me? Believe me, being independent isn't all it's cracked up to be. I would love to be able to depend on someone the way you depend on me, but I don't have that luxury. I must be independent and, frankly, it gets lonely."

She either wasn't getting what I was trying to say or didn't want to understand it. "While I'm gone for the next month or so, you should take some time for yourself. You don't do much of that. Take a vacation."

"I thought you just told me that you need me to take care of things here for you while you're gone."

I had said that. "You can figure out how to do what needs to be done around here while also taking some time off. You know, I gave you that house in Miami so that you could go there and chill every now and then. When's the last time you were out there?"

"It has been a while," she admitted. "But I don't know if I want to go out there right now."

"You know, if you don't want that house, I can take that one back and give you another one someplace you do like."

"No!" she said quickly. "I love that home. Please, don't take it back."

"How can you say that you love that home when you haven't been there in years? I'll take it back and give you another one somewhere you do like. Besides, I miss going to Miami in the summer."

"Jag, please. I will go to Miami while you're in Germany. I do love the place. I don't want a house anywhere else."

"Good. While you're there, lay out and get some sun." She was as pale as a ghost from working inside all the time.

"Okay. I'll do that. I'll spend a week out there. I'll get things handled here, then I'll have free time to just chill out. It'll be fun."

"You should ask one of your girlfriends to go with you. That way, it'll be more fun for you than if you go alone."

Her eyes moved to stare at the floor. "No, that's okay."

"You know, I didn't even think about this, but do you have any girlfriends around Dallas? Are they all back in Sacramento?" She and my mother used to have a huge circle of girlfriends. I'd just assumed she still had tons of them.

Nodding, she said, "Yeah, they're all back home. Working for you hasn't given me much time to myself. Most of the women I was friends with were the people I worked with. Being an assistant to you hasn't given me any coworkers with whom I could become friendly."

That sounded lonely to me. "You can see if any of your old friends want to fly out and join you in Miami when you go. However many you want. Use the company credit card to fly them in. Have a party. Enjoy life, Miss Petty. Don't let anything that has to do with me stop you from doing you."

"I'll do that. Thanks for bringing it up. Now, won't you consider letting Sean have this chance to go with you to Germany?"

"Are you serious right now? I said no, and I'm going to stick with that answer."

"It's just that I really do think it would be safer if someone was with you. I don't want to have to worry about you the whole time you're gone."

She reminded me of my mother. "Miss Petty, I know you think you need to watch out for me."

"Good, then you will take Sean with you. Your mother would be telling you the same thing if she were still here."

Damn it! Why did she have to go there?

Chapter Eighteen

Millie

It took two days to drive to Miami from Shiner. Stopping overnight to spend the night in a hotel in Gulfport, Mississippi, Myra and I were both so tired that we slept like the dead until my alarm went off and we had to get up to meet the driver back at the car to take off again.

The whole thing was on the awkward side. Samantha had directed the driver not to speak to us too much. She'd called me when the driver was parked outside our apartment, instructing me not to give him my phone number or say our names in his presence. She didn't want anyone to know where Myra and I were going or who we were.

Needless to say, my sister and I had stayed quiet, entertaining ourselves with our cell phones during the long ride to our new home. And when we stopped in front of a building so great that it seemed as if I had to be dreaming, my sister and I found ourselves truly speechless.

The driver popped the trunk and we grabbed our two garbage bags, then walked in slow motion toward the front door. Framed with the biggest green potted plants I'd ever seen, the white door shone like a beacon of light, pulling us into the home's warm embrace. We stood in the entrance area as the driver drove off. "Put the code in, Millie," Myra urged me.

"I'm sort of in shock right now."

"So am I. Let's be in shock on the inside of this place instead of outside of it, though ."

Tapping in the code Samantha had given me, I heard the door unlock. Then I turned the handle, opening the door. "Oh, my..."

"God," Myra finished what I'd started. "No way. There is no possible way we are meant to live here. It's too much, Millie. Way too much."

This did not look like a home. It looked like something out of a magazine. Everything sparkled and shone like diamonds. The furnishings, covered in different types of white fabrics, looked too expensive for us to sit on. "Everything is white, Myra. Let's not sit down anywhere. Maybe we can find some part of this home that we can actually relax in."

"Your baby won't be easy to raise in a home like this. It's too perfect. If we don't ruin this place, the baby will." She stepped forward, taking one slow step at a time.

We went from the living room into the next room, which seemed to be the real living area. "Holy shit! That thing back there was just the entrance room—or whatever they call the smaller living room that leads to the bigger one."

Two large sectionals, done in rustic leather, ran along opposite walls, acting like parentheses that surrounded pure excellence. A chandelier hung from the cathedral ceiling. It wasn't even turned on, but still sparkled from the sunlight that trickled in through the wall of glass that made up the outer wall.

"It looks like a tropical paradise out of that window, Millie. Can this be real?"

"We are in Miami. I suppose it's to be expected." We went to the window, looking out over what seemed to be the backyard. A swimming pool, complete with a diving board and a slide, was the main focal point. "We can swim any time we want."

She put down the garbage bag full of bathroom stuff and turned to me. "Put that down, and let's explore our new home, Millie. It seems like this could take a while, and I don't want to lug around this stupid bag."

I put mine down too and off we went, looking into every nook and cranny, finding room after room of fine furnishings and glorious views. And then we found a door that led us into the garage. "The cars."

Myra nodded as the lights came on when I opened the door. "Those are the nicest cars I've ever seen. I'm glad I got my driver's license last month." She went straight to the bright red one. "I'll take this little beauty."

"That's a corvette, and you are *not* going to be driving that." I couldn't let her get behind the wheel of something as powerful as that thing. "How about we share the Lincoln over there?"

"That's a grandma car," she said, shaking her head. "I like this one. It looks fast."

"I'm sure it is fast. But you and I ain't gonna be driving that thing anywhere. What if we wreck it?" I wasn't going to be responsible for something that had to have cost more than my life was worth. "The Lincoln is very nice, and it's much safer too."

"Party pooper."

"So, I think I'll take the bedroom at the very end of the hallway."

"I guess I'll take the one closest to that one because I'm kind of scared to be too far away from you in this big house. Since we're in the kitchen, let's take a look around to see if there's anything to eat in this place."

"I doubt there is. Samantha said she hasn't been here in ages." But when I opened the fridge, I found it full of all sorts of things. "What the hell?"

"She's had it stocked for us!" Opening cabinet after cabinet, she found more food than our local grocery store back home had in stock. "We will never need to go grocery shopping again with all this stuff." She took out a box of Kraft Mac and Cheese. "Look, it's the real stuff, not the store brand. It's like we're royalty or something."

"There's an entire freezer the same size as the fridge," I said with a gasp. "And it's full of all kinds of meats."

We were set for a very long time. "She said that we won't have to worry about money, and it seems like she wasn't playing around."

"Hey, I wonder if the bathrooms are fully stocked too. I didn't even go through any of the cabinets in any of them." Myra took off like a shot to find out what lay hidden in the many bathrooms.

I tried to figure out what I wanted to cook with so much at my disposal. While pulling a pot roast out of the freezer, I remembered that Samantha had said to text her when we arrived.

Pulling out my phone, I sent her a text to let her know we'd made it. She called me right away. "Hi, Samantha. What a home you have here. My sister and I are a little overwhelmed with how wonderful it is."

"Don't be. It's just a house. How was the trip?"

"Long."

"Yes. I know that the drive is too much longer than if you'd taken a plane. But I couldn't risk buying you two the tickets. The maid service comes once a week on Mondays. I think it would be best for you two to be away from the house on Mondays so that you don't interact with any of the staff. We can't have anyone knowing your names."

I wasn't sure I liked that. "So, we can't really get to know anyone here?"

"No," came her quick and blunt answer. "You've got a little slice of paradise right there. There's plenty to keep you girls occupied right there in the house.

On Mondays, you two can go out and shop, dine out, go to the beach, whatever you want. Just don't tell people your real names while you're out and about. And don't say a thing about where you really come from. Make something up. But mostly, try not to speak too much to anyone. It's just safer that way."

"You know Myra has to go to school, right?"

"I've already thought about that. There are online high schools. Enroll her in one of those. I'll send you a picture of the credit card that you can use to pay the tuition."

Seemed she'd thought about everything. Except my pregnancy. "I'll need to start seeing a doctor, you know."

"There are midwife services in the area that you can use instead of a formal doctor. You can have the baby right there in the house, and the midwife will come to see you for the prenatal visits."

"What about the birth certificate and things like that? My name will have to be on those things."

"I'm looking into getting your names changed."

That was going too far. "You know, our names are all we have left of our parents. Jag isn't going to look for us in Miami. I think we'll be just fine. I don't think we need to become a couple of recluses either."

"For now, please do as I say. You don't want to lose that precious little angel, do you?"

"For now." There was no way I could live the way she wanted. And I wouldn't ask my sister to live that way either. Not for an extended period, anyway.

"Now, about the pregnancy," she said. "If you lose the baby, then this arrangement is over. You understand that, right?"

I didn't even want to think about losing my baby. "I suppose I understood that. But I haven't thought about something like that happening. And I don't want to think about it either."

"Of course you don't want to think about that. But it does sometimes happen."

"So, I should hang on to as much of the money you give me as I can, in case I need to go back home."

"I didn't say that. Spend the money I send you. If something happens, then I'll pay to send you two back to where you came from. Or wherever you might want to go."

So, the home wasn't permanent. "I'll keep that in mind. Thanks for helping us out, Samantha. It's very nice of you. But what are you getting from this? No offense. I don't mean to say you've got anything to gain by doing this."

"You are a woman. And so am I. I just would hate to see him hurt you or the baby. That's all. Let's just say that I've got a big heart."

"One of the biggest." I couldn't help feeling guilty about keeping the baby from Jag, though. "And what if I decide that I want to take the risk and tell Jag about our baby, then what?"

"You would hate yourself if you did something like that. I cannot emphasize that enough."

"I know you think he'll take me to court so that he can get custody of our baby. But I don't think there's a judge alive who would agree with him. I've never been in any trouble. There would be no reason to take my baby."

"There's no judge alive who doesn't like money. You need to remember that Jag has more than enough money to buy off any judge so that he can get what he wants. He can hire lawyers, and even if you saved every dime I give you, you wouldn't have enough to hire one that's as good as his."

"He already has lawyers?" I found that a little weird. "For what?"

"He keeps them on retainer. In other words, he's got his pitbulls in their kennels, ready to attack when prompted. And he will set them lose on you if he wants what you have. I've seen him do it before."

"You might've seen him do it in the business world, but on a human?" I couldn't see him being that heartless. "A little baby?"

"It's his," she stated with frankness in her voice. "The baby is his. That's the way he will think about it. He won't think that it's both of yours. His brain doesn't work that way—he shares nothing."

"Are you sure?" I just couldn't believe he was the monster she painted him out to be.

"You know, you don't have to take my charity. You can do whatever you want. I'm not making you take what I'm offering. I'm only doing this for your sake. You have the freedom to do as you wish. But I know that you will regret it if you tell him a thing about this pregnancy."

I had to keep my baby safe. "For now, I'm going to listen to you. But if I decide that I need to tell him about our baby, I'll leave your home and any money that's left, and I'll do what my heart tells me to do."

"That would be a mistake, but it's up to you. I will make sure you're taken care of for as long as you need me. This is a long-term commitment that I'm making to you. Just remember that whenever you think that you should tell Jag about this. I will keep you and your family safe and financially taken care of. He will strip you of everything you hold dear."

A chill ran through me with her words. I didn't know the man the way she did. It bothered me that I'd fallen for him even a little bit in the short amount of time we'd spent together. It made me wonder if I had any sense at all when it came to the opposite sex.

"Thank you, Samantha. I've always had bad luck with the guys I've gone out with. Maybe I shouldn't trust my judgment. I'm going to keep this baby safe and with me. Thanks to you."

"It's my privilege to help you. Any woman worth her salt would do the same."

She was so wrong about that. "No, you're special."

"Aww, that's sweet of you to say. You two settle in, make yourselves at home. I'll be in touch. And you can always text if you need me. One more thing."

"Yes?"

"Drive that Corvette. It's a life-changing experience."

"Oh, I don't think I can do that."

"Do it. I'm serious. It will change how you look at the world. Life has so much more to offer than you think. Have fun. I know you and your sister haven't had much of that. But keep your names secret. Don't forget to do that."

"Will do. Thanks again. Bye."

Just as our call ended, Myra came back into the kitchen. "I don't think we're ever going to have to buy toilet paper again. Or any toiletry either. This place is stocked up to the max."

"I just talked to Samantha. We're to keep our real names and where we come from a secret."

"I thought as much."

"And she said we should take the Corvette for a drive. She said it's life-changing."

"Then what are we waiting for?" she shouted, sprinting toward the garage.

The only thing I'm waiting for is the other shoe to drop. This is all way too good to be true.

Chapter Nineteen

Jag

I couldn't stop thinking about Millie and worrying about her. So, I took off the very next morning to make the four-hour drive to Shiner. I wasn't going to just take Miss Petty's word for it. I had to find things out for myself.

Pulling into town, I went right to the diner. As soon as I walked in the waitresses looked my way, and one of them shouted, "It's you!"

I recognized Rachel instantly. "Hey, Rachel. How's it been going?"

Racing toward me, she asked, "Is she with you?"

"Millie?" I asked.

Shaking her head, she said, "Yeah, Millie. We've all been so worried about her. Our best guess was that she ran off with you. So, where is she?"

"I'm sorry to say that she's not with me."

"But she left with you, didn't she?"

"No, I'm afraid not. I'm actually here to find out if anyone knows about where she went. I've been worried about her."

"Us too," she said as she looked at the other waitresses. "It wasn't like her to just tape a note to the door of the diner after everyone had left. And your assistant, that older lady, had been here earlier that same day. We all thought that she'd come to tell Millie that you wanted her to go with you somewhere, and that's where she and her sister went later that night."

Something wasn't adding up. "Hang on. Are you saying that Millie saw my assistant when she came here two months ago?"

"Yeah, she saw her. They talked in the back for a bit. Millie was acting so strange that day. Even before your assistant showed up. Millie had just taken off—vanished right at the lunch rush. And for the first time in a long time, we'd actually been super busy, so her disappearing left us in a lurch."

Something wasn't right. "I did send my assistant here two months ago to ask Millie and her sister if they would come to Dallas to join me at my place for the weekend. And when my assistant called me, I asked her what Millie had said."

Rachel led the way to a nearby table, where we sat down. "What did she tell you?"

"Miss Petty said that Millie had left town. And no one knew where she went."

"You're saying that your assistant called you the same day she came here and talked to Millie? Like, during the daytime?" she asked with worry-filled eyes.

"Yes, that day. It was still light outside. I'd said there was no way Millie would've done something like that. So, I asked if she was just screwing with me."

"She wasn't telling you the truth. Not at that time anyway. Millie left later that night, though."

"Miss Petty had said rather sternly that she would never do that. She stated flatly that Millie had moved away."

"See, none of us could understand why Millie left, unless she'd left with you. That would've been the only thing that would've made any sense at all. But most of us thought that she or her sister would've called at least one of us to say hi, if nothing else."

"I'd told my assistant that Millie wouldn't have left town without saying a word to anyone. She has no one. The people here are like her family. She wouldn't leave you guys. And that's when I asked about her sister."

Rachel seemed intrigued as she propped her elbows on the table and leaned forward. "What would that woman know about Millie's sister?"

"She said that they were both gone. From what Millie's coworkers had told her. She said that you guys told her that Millie had left a note on the door of the diner, saying that she and her sister had moved and wouldn't be coming back."

"Funny how that hadn't happened yet, isn't it?" she asked with a smirk.

"So, there's no way that Millie did that?"

"Not at that time, no."

I told my assistant that you guys must've been lying. I asked her to go to Millie's apartment to see if she was there or if she could ask the landlord whether she had moved or not. I told my assistant that I could imagine Millie's friends and coworkers lying about her whereabouts, but I doubted her landlord would lie."

"Did she say she would go over there?" Rachel asked.

"No. My assistant said that if Millie had gone to those lengths to avoid me, then why would I even want anything else to do with her?"

"First of all, Millie isn't a coward like that. She wouldn't ask us to lie for her. She would tell you straight up if she didn't want anything to do with you."

"Yeah, I thought the same thing. If she had done something that low, then I felt sure that I wouldn't want anything to do with her anyway. But I could not believe that Millie would move away like that without telling anyone a thing about it. And I still can't believe that she wouldn't have told anyone where she was going. I just can't believe any of this. With all I've learned here, I think there's every reason in the world to be worried about her."

"Me too," Rachel agreed. "But it's been two months since that happened, Jag. Why are you only coming to look for her now?"

"Miss Petty told me that Millie was a grown woman, and that I didn't need to worry about her. She said that I didn't really know Millie and that I shouldn't make a judgment call like that when I had only spent a handful of hours with her."

"But you *do* know her. Millie's sort of an open book," Rachel said. "Well, up until she took her sister and left town that night."

"I did feel like I knew her well enough to know that she wouldn't just take off without telling anyone why she was doing it and where she was going. I speculated that maybe the two of them had been kidnapped."

"Oh, God!" Fear filled Rachel's face. "Do you really think something like that might've happened?"

"I'm not sure of anything anymore. Miss Petty even told me that she'd talked to you, Rachel," I recalled, now that I'd immersed myself in the conversation she and I had months ago. "She said that you speculated that she might have run off with an old boyfriend. She said that you had said that Millie might not have wanted anyone to know about her returning to one of her old flames, and that's why she left town without telling anyone."

Shaking her head, she said, "That conversation never happened. What the actual fuck is going on, Jag?"

A chill ran through me as I remembered something else Miss Petty had said during that conversation. "Miss Petty told me that Millie was gone and that it was highly doubtful she and I would ever cross paths again."

"Jag, that sounds bad."

Nodding, I agreed. "Very bad. When I brought up ways I might be able to track her down, like checking with her sister's school and talking to you guys' boss to ask if anyone had called him to ask about a reference for Millie in case she had found a job wherever she'd gone, she told me it was illegal for any of them to give me information on their staff or students."

"You should've called the diner anyway," Rachel said.

Nodding, I said, "I told her that I was going to call the diner anyway. And she asked me what if my instincts were right and Millie had told you guys to say that she had moved? Miss Petty said that I would feel terrible if that was the case and to just let it go."

"So, you let it go so that you wouldn't get your feelings hurt?" Rachel asked with a frown.

"I argued with Miss Petty, asking what if something had happened to Millie, then what?"

"What did she tell you?"

"She said that if something had happened to Millie, then how would I even find that out? I asked if any of Millie's friends had tried calling her."

"We all have. And we've all tried calling Myra's phone too. Neither of them will answer our calls. They send them straight to voicemail. And we've left numerous messages too."

"I said that maybe I should call the police here in Shiner. But Miss Petty told me that I sounded like a crazy person. I asked where Millie could've gotten the money to move in the first place. I mean, she didn't even have a car. Did she walk away?"

"We all thought the same things you did, Jag."

"Was Millie an honest person?" I had to ask.

"Yes, she was brutally honest at times," Rachel confirmed.

"I thought so too, but Miss Petty said that Millie might just be a huge liar."

"She was not!" Rachel said, sounding super pissed.

"Miss Petty told me that none of you guys even seemed worried about Millie and how abruptly she'd left."

"Well, that's a lie," Rachel said.

"Yeah, but I didn't know that at the time. So, I began to think that I was overreacting and that I needed to stop."

"Now I feel bad." She rubbed her forehead. "We had all pretty much decided that she and Myra were with you, and we had pretty much stopped worrying. But she isn't with you, and your assistant has been lying to you about things. I don't know about you, Jag, but I smell a huge rat."

"She's never made me question a thing before," I said. My world seemed to be spinning out of control. "I've known her since I was a kid. She was my mom's best friend. She was there for me when Mom first got diagnosed with breast cancer. And when Mom passed, it was Miss Petty who held my hand, hugged me, and told me things were going to be okay."

"I hate to say this, but maybe she did something to Millie and her sister because she thought she might lose you," Rachel suggested.

I looked at her, wondering if that could even be true. "Lose me? How would she lose me? She's my assistant. Like, for personal and business things. And she's someone I confide in too. How would me having a relationship with Millie get in the way of that?"

"Maybe she wants more, Jag. You're a good-looking man with lots of things going for you."

"No way. She has never acted like she wanted anything more from me. And that's just gross. She's my mom's best friend. That's just so—well, yuck."

"I agree." She nodded. "But things like that can happen. You did say that you sent her here to ask Millie to spend time with you. That might have made her jealous."

"She didn't act jealous. Not even a little."

"She didn't want you guys together."

Looking at her, I had to ask, "How do you know that?" I hadn't told Millie anything that Miss Petty had told me.

"Millie went to see you at the RV before you guys left."

"She did?" I'd had no idea she'd done that. "No one told me she did that."

"Well, she did. I was the one who had talked her into going to talk to you, so when she came back from there, she was mad at me for butting into her life."

"Why was that?"

"Because of the things your assistant said to her," she said. "That's why."

"Did she tell you anything about what was said between them?"

"Yes, she did. Well, she yelled at me the things that were said. She was super pissed at me. She said that your assistant knew that you had spent the night with her."

"Yeah, I tell Miss Petty pretty much everything. But not like sex stuff."

"Yeah." She rolled her eyes. "Anyway, your assistant went on to say that you and she were very close and that you tell her everything. Millie was a little surprised that you hadn't mentioned your assistant to her, though."

"I saw no reason to, is why I didn't do that," I let her know.

"Well, it made Millie feel kind of bad that this woman knew everything, even her first and last name, and yet Millie knew nothing about her. When your assistant told Millie that she wasn't in your league and that she was sure Millie already knew that, she was hurt. She also told Millie that she'd done the right thing telling you that it was best for you two to part ways without trying to stay connected by anything." She blinked a few times as she looked at me. "For real though, you told your assistant all those details, Jag?"

"I did do that." But now I felt stupid for doing it. I would have never imagined Miss Petty doing something like that.

"So, your assistant went on to tell Millie that she could never be what you need. That your worlds had collided only briefly, and she should be happy with what she got from you but not to expect anything else. And then your trusted assistant said that you were going to break Millie's heart. She even brought up the fact that Millie's parents are dead. You even told that woman *that*, Jag. How could you?"

"I wish I knew. I won't be making that mistake again, I can tell you that." I felt like I didn't even know that woman at all. "Was that everything she said to Millie?"

"Nope. Your assistant went on to say things about you that weren't too nice. Things like she'd seen you in action, whatever that means. And that you never stayed in relationships for long. You move really fast, and then you're like, on to the next thing. She even told Millie that if you were into her, then why would you be leaving town so fast?"

"I wanted to spend more time with Millie. It was Miss Petty who sent me on my way. Did she tell you that?"

"Yes. And that's exactly why I urged Millie to go and talk to you to fix that stupid crap she'd said. She can be her own worst enemy at times."

"I've made some big mistakes."

"Can you fix them?" she asked. "Can you find Millie?"

"I'm going to try."

"You need to start with asking your assistant what she really knows about all this and tell her that you know she's lied to you. Jag, you've got to find Millie and her sister. You have to do it. Make that woman talk."

How could I not have seen Miss Petty's true colors all these years?

Chapter Twenty

Millie

I sat on one of the many luxurious sofas in Samantha's home, running my hand over my still-flat stomach, wondering when the first signs of a baby bump would begin to appear. I was now in my third month, the end of the first trimester. From what I'd been finding online about pregnancy, things were about to really change with my body.

I'd learned which new things happened with the baby and my body each week. At least I had the good luck to know the exact date I'd gotten pregnant. That left me knowing exactly what week I was in.

Currently, I was in week twelve—the last week of my first trimester. Most women didn't do too well in the first trimester. I'd been one of the lucky ones, thank goodness. I'd had no morning sickness at all. At least, not so far.

The baby I carried was supposed to be around two inches long now and would begin to move around a lot soon. The fetus looked like a real baby, and it was beginning to do things like suck its thumb. That sounded crazy to me.

I had this tiny human growing inside me. I'd never even really given having a baby much thought before. I had always figured I would have kids one day, after I found a man I fell in love with and maybe even married.

Who knew it would be this easy to get pregnant?

So far, everything about the pregnancy had been easy. But what was coming next might be problematic for me. From what I'd read, I might begin to experience an enhanced libido. Which meant that I might begin to crave sex. And—being a single woman—that could be a problem, making me feel sexual frustration to a degree I never had before.

So, I tried not to kick myself for the thoughts that had begun to run through my head. Thoughts about Jag, for one.

I'd done as Samantha had recommended for the last couple of months. Although I wasn't quite sure that she did have an agenda of keeping me and Jag apart, I didn't want to take a chance on losing my baby to the man.

She'd said some things about him that I hadn't thought could possibly be true. But I had to remind myself that I'd known the man for less than twenty-four hours, so who was I to say Samantha was lying?

I saw no reason, other than trying to help me, for her to go to so much trouble and expense to take care of me and my sister. But so far she hadn't done a thing for the baby I carried.

She'd said that she wanted me to use a midwife. But when I began checking them out and telling her about them, she told me to wait until I was past the twelve-week mark because the chances of losing the fetus prior to that time were on the high side.

It was a relief to me that I'd made it to this point. Now, I could begin letting myself enjoy the pregnancy and think about the baby's future a lot more than I had before.

Names came to mind. Of course, my mother's and father's names stuck inside my head. And then there was Jag's mother, who'd also passed away. Our baby would grow up without any grandparents. I found that sad.

Not that my sister and I had many years with our grandparents. By the time I was ten, all four of them had passed away. And I had no idea if Jag had known his mother's parents or not. We hadn't had much time to talk before he'd left town.

I should've called him that day.

I'd let Samantha get inside my head that morning. My pride was hurt and insecurities had really set in. But I still should've called him.

Jumping as my cell rang, I picked the phone up off the coffee table in front of me. I thought it was funny that I'd been doing so much thinking about Jag, and now Samantha was calling me. "Hello, Samantha. How's your day going?"

"It's going fine. Listen, Jag is going to Germany next week, and he'll be gone for a couple of months. He wants me to take some vacation time. He was the one who gave me the house in Miami. When I told him that I didn't need a vacation, he told me he would sell the Miami home and buy me something in a place that I would want to visit more often."

"He said he would sell it?" I thought that did sound kind of mean.

"Yes. So, I told him that I would spend some time there so that he wouldn't sell the place. That way, you and your sister won't have to be moved again. He can be so tyrannical."

It sure sounded like that. "So, you're coming here? When?"

"In about two weeks. He's leaving next week. I've got some things to do here in Dallas, and then I'll come to Miami. I just wanted to make sure that neither you or your sister was using the bedroom I use when I'm there."

"Which one is it?"

"The one at the end of the hall. I had the maid service put my personal things in the attic before you got there. The door to the attic is inside the linen closet in the attached bathroom. I'm going to give them instructions to put my things back out in that room on Monday when they come to clean."

"Okay." I had been using that room as mine but didn't want to admit that to her. "I can put your things out if you want."

"No. Someone from the maid service put them up for me, so they know where the things belong. No need for you to do any work, Millie."

"How long will you be staying?" I asked. "Like, are you going to have enough time to help me find a good midwife while you're here?"

"Yes, I can do that. I'm going to stay for a week before going to the house in Los Angeles, where I'll stay a week or so to take care of things over there. I'll move around from place to place while Jag's out of the country, so I can take care of all he's left me in charge of."

Her job sounded super hard. "He's lucky he has you, Samantha. It sounds like you do the work of many assistants."

"I do. But the pay is worth it."

Looking around the posh room I sat in, it was obvious that she made an impressive amount of money as his assistant. "Well, it'll be good to see you. Travel safe."

"Thank you. See you then."

Getting up, I went to the bedroom I'd made my own only to find out that it was really the one Samantha called her own. Curiosity got to me as I went into the attached bathroom, then to the linen closet where she said her personal things had been stored in the attic.

I pulled over the chair that went with the vanity so that I could climb up to open the attic door. As soon as I got it open and the stairs unfolded to the floor, I saw a box at the top and went up to get it.

It wasn't like me to be so nosy, but I couldn't seem to stop myself from seeing what she'd had hidden in the attic before our arrival.

As I pulled the box toward me, taking it into my arms and then moving back down the stairs, I felt the slightest twinge of guilt for looking through her personal things. But then another emotion rushed through me—one of distrust.

Since I didn't know either Samantha or Jag well at all, how could I know if one of them could be trusted? Maybe there was something in Samantha's personal belongings that would help me make a better decision than the ones I'd made so far.

Myra and I were grateful for what Samantha had done for us. Letting us live in her home, drive her cars, eat her expensive food—those were things that were amazing beyond belief, and we were happy to be able to have them. But the seclusion, the secrets, and the fact we couldn't call each other by our real names while out in public didn't make us happy at all.

If Jag were a real threat to the baby I carried, then Myra and I were prepared to live life on the secretive side for however long we had to. Protecting the baby was the most important thing to both of us.

But if there was no reason to worry about Jag taking the baby away from me, then all this was for nothing. It would just be something that would eventually hurt Jag when he found out what I'd done.

Placing the box on the bed, I took the lid off and found Ziplock baggies with picture frames in them. Each picture was in a separate bag, and each one had Jag as the main character of the photo.

I couldn't help myself. Seeing his handsome face made my heart do flips inside my chest. I pulled the first picture out and held it against my heart. "Tell me that all she's said about you isn't true, Jag." I so did not want to believe Samantha about the type of person that he was. But not listening to her was too big of a risk.

Pulling the framed photo away from my chest, I gazed at the picture of the man who'd given me the greatest gift a man can give a woman. A baby.

My heart ached as I looked at him. I wished like hell that the picture could give me some insight into the man he really was. His genuine smile made me think that his heart was good.

But what if I'm wrong and Samantha is right?

Putting that picture down on the bed, I took out the next one, finding Jag wearing snow skies with a soft, white blanket of snow in the background, dark sunglasses, and that stunning smile on his lips.

How can that man be so evil that he would take a baby away from its mother?

It was impossible for me to look at these pictures and see anything but good in him. One after the other showed his bright smile and how he must've loved to have fun. He enjoyed life, from what the pictures said about him.

I laid them all out on the bed, standing to look at them all, when I heard Myra clearing her throat. "Um, what the heck is this, Millie?"

"Pictures of Jag."

"Damn, he's hot! But where did you get all these?"

I pointed at the now empty box. "It was tucked away in the attic."

"Okay. And how did you find them?"

"Samantha called a little while ago. She told me that she's coming in two weeks to stay for a week. She said the maid service would be getting her things out of the attic. And the door to it was at the top of the linen closet. So, I went up there and found these."

"If she said the maid service was going to get them out, then why did you do that?" She picked up a picture of Jag and looked at it. "This man is the father of your baby?"

"He is."

"This kid is going to have some amazing genes."

"Jag's mother was artificially inseminated by an anonymous sperm donor. So, I bet Jag does come from an amazing gene pool if his mother was able to pick from the genetics she liked."

"That's um, well, weird really," Myra said. "And you told me that his mother died from cancer. So, he doesn't have anyone anymore."

I put my hand on my stomach. "He's got this little one."

"That he can't ever know about."

I wasn't sure if that's how things would be or not. "I'm having some unsure feelings about that."

Her eyes scanned all the pictures. "There are ten of them."

"And he looks happy in all of them. He looks nice—sweet even. I can't find anything in any of his expressions that makes me think that he could be as bad as Samantha says he is."

"I agree. But you're not really finding the obvious super-creepy sign that I am." Placing her hand on my shoulder, she asked, "Don't you think that this man's assistant having this many framed pictures of him is weird?"

"This is her bedroom," I said. "I didn't know that until today."

"So, you found out that this is her bedroom, and she had these pictures hidden in the attic?"

"She had the maid service put them up there right before we came here." My mind began to run away with me. "You don't think that she didn't want me to know that she had these pictures of Jag in her bedroom, do you?"

"Well, she obviously didn't want you to know about them, or she wouldn't have had them put away like that. But then she alerted you about them and where they were."

"Well, she didn't know that I would go up there and get them. She told me not to." As I looked at all the pictures that lay on her bed, I began to feel sick to my stomach.

Running to the bathroom, I threw up in the toilet, holding my stomach as pain radiated through it. When I stood, I found my sister standing there with a wet washcloth in her hand. "Here. Wash your face with this. When Haley from my Spanish class was pregnant, she kept a wet washcloth with her for after throwing up. I'm surprised this is the first time you're doing this since the start of the pregnancy."

"I don't think it's from the pregnancy. I think it's from me feeling guilty, stupid, and slightly disgusted with both Samantha and myself."

"Have you begun to see her in a different light? Maybe a green-tinged light that surrounds her like some evil cloud? You know, a jealous light?"

"I can see no other reason for her to have framed pictures of Jag that she has kept in her bedroom for God only knows how long other than having a romantic interest in the man she works for. But what's worse—she's known him since he was a kid."

Can I be reading this right? Or am I completely off here?

Chapter Twenty-One

Jag

Miss Petty had straight-up lied to me about Millie. *But why?*

After the conversation I'd had with Rachel, I had jumped into my car, heading back to Dallas to confront my assistant in person. I'd driven like a demon, getting back in record time. Just as I pulled into the garage, my cell rang, and I saw her name on the screen. "Hey," I answered Miss Petty's call. "Where are you right now?"

"On my way to the spa to get some much-needed pampering. I'm calling you to ask where you are."

"I just pulled into the garage at home. I need you to come back here so that we can talk."

"About what?" she asked, sounding innocent, which she was not.

"Just come back here, and you can find out. I'm not doing this over the phone."

"You sound angry," she pointed out. "Why would you be angry?"

"I'll tell you when you get here."

"Tell me now. Are you angry with me for some reason?"

"Just come here, and we can talk."

"Jag, does this have anything to do with wherever you disappeared to?"

"Look, I am not doing this over the phone. Just get back here." Swiping the screen, I ended the call before stomping into the house.

I heard the sound of the house phone as it rang and then the muffled sound of the chef, who was working in the kitchen, as he answered the call. I didn't care who was calling. I only cared about getting to the bottom of where Millie was. And I knew that my assistant had something to do with it.

Sitting in the foyer where I knew she would come in first, I waited, trying my best to calm down so that I didn't come off as crazy. But it wasn't going to be easy to pull off. I was insanely pissed.

"Jag," I heard the chef calling out. "Where have you gotten off to?"

"I'm in the foyer, James."

He came in, a drink in his hand. "Miss Petty called and asked me to bring you a drink. She said you sounded upset when she talked to you." He placed the drink on the table next to me. "Would you care to talk to me about it?"

"No." I picked up the drink, taking a long drink. "But thank you for the drink. I do need to calm down before I speak to her. She's supposed to be on her way back here. Do you know how long ago she left?"

"Not really. I've been busy in the kitchen."

"Well, thanks for the drink, James. You can get back to your work. I'm just going to sit here until she shows up."

"If you don't mind me saying, you seem very agitated. What in the world could Miss Petty have done to upset you this much?"

"I don't want to spread rumors. Something that she may have had a hand in just came to my attention, and I want to find out what she knows."

"Okay. I'll get back to work."

I'd downed the whole alcoholic drink before she finally walked into the house. "Oh, you're right here." Her eyes were as big as saucers. "Should we go to your office to talk?"

"Here's fine." I stood. "You sit."

"Jag, really. Let's just talk in the office where we won't be overheard."

"You like to lead. And I've let you do that. I've let it go on for too long. I can see that now. You think you know what's best for me and won't listen to what I want. I want to do this right here. Right now. Got it?"

"I just think that you're acting very aggressive, and I don't want any of the staff to see you like this. I don't know what's wrong with you, but we can get to the bottom of this without alerting the entire staff."

"You lied to me."

"Jag, come on." She walked out of the room, not taking a seat the way I'd told her to.

So I followed her to the office where she'd wanted to talk anyway. "Fine, no one can hear us in here." I closed the door behind me. "Tell me why you lied."

"Where did you go today?" She turned to face me, then took a seat on the sofa that ran along the wall of my office. "You should sit. There's really no reason for all this aggressiveness."

I wasn't going to sit and stay like the good boy she was trying to turn me into. "So, you're not even going to say a thing about what I've said? You're not going to even ask me what I'm talking about?"

"I would definitely like to know why you're accusing me of something like that."

"Because you have lied to me. That's why I'm accusing you."

"And when did I supposedly lie to you, Jag?"

"The day I sent you to ask Millie to come to Dallas to spend the weekend with me. That's when you lied to me."

Her eyes moved to the ceiling as she seemed to be trying to bring that memory back to her brain. "Like, a couple of months ago?" She looked at me, shaking her head. "That long ago?"

"Yes, that long ago. You told me that she had already left town without telling anyone where she was going. That was a lie."

"It was not. You can ask anyone if that's what that girl did. I told you the truth," she defended herself.

I had to give it to her—she was going to stick to her story until the very end. But the end was about to come. "Yes, she did leave town exactly the way you said she did. She did leave a note on the diner's door after it was closed. Only she did that *after* your visit to Shiner."

"If anyone told you that, they are the ones who have lied to you, Jag. Not me."

"Rachel said she never spoke to you."

"And who is that?"

"Well, she's the waitress who worked with Millie who you said told you about Millie's leaving town without telling anyone a thing. Funny, you can't even recall that woman."

With a huff, Miss Petty crossed her arms over her chest, puffing up as if she was angry now. "Look, I'm not lying to you. Millie isn't in Shiner anymore."

"Then where is she?" I would not let her out of my sight until she told me the truth. "You will tell me where she is because I know that you know exactly where that is. You know that because you orchestrated her leaving her hometown without telling a soul."

"I had nothing to do with that."

"The fuck you haven't." I would not let her get away with this. "Tell me why you would do something so devious."

Her jaw tightened—I knew she was mad as hell. "Look, I got to Shiner. I saw her. I saw all of them. Not even one of those shitty waitresses are going anywhere with their lives. And there you were, wanting me to help you get one of those low-life do-nothing girls to spend the weekend with you. And I could not stomach the thought."

"It wasn't up to you."

"I'm not only your assistant. I'm your mother's best friend. And I made a promise to her to look out for you. So I could not, with any good intentions, tell that girl that you wanted to be with her."

"So, what did you tell her?"

Looking away, it was obvious that she didn't want to tell me what she'd said to Millie to get her to leave the only people she really knew. "I might have told her that you weren't a good person."

For a moment, I thought I'd heard her wrong. "You said that I'm not a good person?"

"Yes." She looked me in the eyes. "I told her that you were going to come to Shiner to coax her into coming to Dallas and that you wouldn't let her or her sister leave once you got her here."

Like a dagger had been plunged into my back, I took a couple of steps back, reeling from what she said. "You told her that?"

"I wanted to scare her. I wanted to make sure that you couldn't find her. She is nothing but trash, Jag. She's not the woman for you. I could see it in your eyes. You were going to give her more than she deserves."

"That's not up to you. I have to talk to her. You know how I can contact her. I know you do."

"I don't. I told her those things, and then she told me that she had to get out of there. And I agreed with her. But that's all I did."

I wasn't stupid. "Millie had no money to leave town. She had no car. And no one there would've given her either of those things. Otherwise, someone would've known why she left and even where she was going."

With a shrug, she said, "I can't say how she pulled off leaving, but she did it somehow. Now, that's all I know. You have the truth. I told her those things to save you from yourself."

A thought occurred to me, and I asked, "Have you done this often?"

"I haven't needed to. She's the first trashy girl you've ever been interested in."

"Calling her trashy isn't fair. It's not her fault that her parents died and left her to be the sole provider for herself and her sister. She didn't have the luxury of doing more than waitressing in that small town. Her time was coming, though. Her plan was to make something of herself one day. And I believe that she will do that."

"You see a hot young girl with half a brain. She let you into her pants within hours of knowing you. She's a whore as well as trash. You really should be thanking me for what I did for you."

"You have no idea how much you've fucked up, do you?"

"How have I fucked up? By saving you from a fate worse than death?" She had the audacity to laugh. "Spending more than a couple of days with that girl would've shown you the bullet you dodged. Maybe I should've let you have your time with her. Maybe then you would know, without a doubt, that she's not the girl for you, Jag."

"You know what? You are wrong. I've never thought about anyone the way I think about her. There hasn't been one day that Millie doesn't come to mind. I miss her. You don't seem to care about any of that, though. You think you know what's best for me, but you don't. I won't pretend to know if Millie and I have a future together or not. But I know that I want to get to know her better. I want to spend time with her. And I will do that. If she wants the same thing."

"Obviously, she doesn't. She did leave town after all."

"Yeah, after you told her that I was some sort of bad guy who would hold her and her sister against their will or some shit like that. You must've made her think that I was some sort of stalker slash kidnapper."

"You can paint that picture however you want to. I'm not going to apologize to you for saving you from something you would have deeply regretted."

Sitting with a thud in the nearest chair, I wasn't sure what to do next, but I had to do something. I rubbed my forehead—I was developing a smashing headache that pulsed and pounded all throughout my head.

When a hand moved over my shoulder, I pulled my hand away from my face and saw Miss Petty standing in front of me with a drink in her hand. "Here, have something to calm you down. If you really want me to find where that girl has gone, I'll do it. I never meant to upset you."

Taking the drink from her, I nodded. "Find her." I took a drink, feeling the heat of the liquor as it moved down my throat and into my stomach, settling into a warm spot in my lower abdomen. "Just find her. All I want is to be able to talk to her—tell her that you lied about me."

"I'll do anything that you want me to, Jag. I'll find her. I'll make this right—you'll see. I never meant to hurt you. I just did what I thought your mother would have wanted me to do."

"She wouldn't have interfered in my love life." I took another sip, feeling the heat take the same path the last one had.

"You're probably right about that. Your mother was very much a person who believed in a person's right to make all the mistakes they wanted. I never thought that way, though." She moved across the room to sit at my desk, opening the laptop that sat on it. "Are you feeling better?"

I hadn't even realized how much better I was feeling until she asked that. "Yeah. I guess knowing that I'm going to get to talk to Millie soon is making me feel a lot better than I've felt since leaving her without saying goodbye. Thanks for understanding."

"Sure." She began tapping away on the computer.

I wasn't sure what she could find out about Millie on the internet, but I had to let her go her own route. She'd helped me with every other aspect of my life and business. I had to put my trust in her.

It was sort of my own fault for sending her to ask Millie to spend the weekend with me in the first place. If I had faced my fears of rejection, then this would never have happened. "Hey, I'm sorry for my part in all this."

She looked over the top of the laptop at me. "Thank you for taking some of the responsibility, Jag. That's very mature of you."

"I'm a thirty-five-year-old man. I'm very mature, naturally."

"Yes, you are." She smiled at me, then looked back at the screen. "You look as if you're feeling tired."

"Yeah. I guess I'm finally relaxing."

"You should go and take a nap. I'll come to let you know when I've found something."

Getting up, I stumbled a little. The half-empty glass slipped out of my hand, crashing to the floor and shattering on impact. "Fuck," I said with a slurred voice.

How the fuck did I get drunk so fast?

Chapter Twenty-Two

Millie

Pacing back and forth in the bedroom, I kept looking at the pictures of Jag that lay on the bed. "I can't just not say anything about this to her."

"No, you can't," Myra agreed.

"Having all these pictures in her bedroom has to mean something."

"It sure does. It means she's got it bad for the man. And I can see why too. I mean, come on, he is more than easy on the eyes. He looks like a freaking movie star or something."

Hours had gone by since I'd found the pictures. But I had finally arrived at the conclusion that I had to speak to Samantha about what I'd found.

Taking my cell phone out of my pocket, I made the call. My knees felt weak, so I sat on the edge of the bed as the phone rang.

"Yes, Millie?" she said as she answered my call. "What can I do for you?"

I didn't want to come off as disrespectful. The woman had done a ton for me and my sister. "Um, I'm not sure how to approach this subject."

"What subject would that be?"

"The subject about the relationship you have with Jag," I blurted out.

"I work for the man."

"Yes. And he confides in you. I know that much."

"Yes, he does."

"You've known each other for a long time," I said, not sure of how to go about asking the main question.

"Yes, we have."

"I'm sure you two feel very comfortable with each other."

"We do," she agreed.

"You are only human," I thought I might bring that up so that it wouldn't sound too rough when I got to where I was heading with this stilted conversation.

"Millie, why would you say something like that?"

"Because, as a human, you probably can't look at Jag without seeing his above-average good looks," I said, trying to sound as respectful as possible.

"Jag is quite handsome. Anyone can see that."

"Okay, so after we talked a while ago, I got curious," I admitted.

"You did?"

"Yes, I did. And I went up to the attic and pulled down the box that was up there. It had nothing but framed pictures of Jag in it. And I am assuming that you had all these pictures of him in your bedroom."

"Why would you assume that?"

"Well, you said you had the maid service put your personal things up there, so I thought those things came out of your bedroom."

"The entire house is mine, Millie. Those pictures were scattered around the house, not in my bedroom. I had them removed so that you wouldn't see him and be reminded of how great he looks and make a call to him that might ruin your life."

Since I had the phone on speaker, Myra could hear what Samantha said too, and she shook her head, whispering, "Why does she have pics of him around her house? Doesn't she see enough of him as it is?"

The point was valid, so I asked, "Samantha, you said yourself that you haven't come here much. So, why would you have pictures of your boss all over the place? I mean, unless you had an attraction toward him."

"And if I did, then what?" she snapped at me. "I mean, that's really none of your business."

"Well, the thing is that if you have the hots for Jag, then you might not be thinking very rationally about me and my situation. What I'm trying to say is..."

"I'm not an idiot. You're accusing me of getting rid of you so that he can't find out about you. Everything I've done is for you. If you're too dumb to understand that, it's not my fault."

Myra's eyes bugged out of her head. "Are you gonna let her talk to you like that?"

I sure was not. "Samantha, I'm trying to be super respectful to you right now, and you're being sort of a..."

"A bitch," Myra said out loud. "She's being a bitch to you, Millie."

"Yeah, that," I agreed. "I would like to talk about this as the adults that we are."

"There's nothing to talk about. You snooped after I told you that I didn't want you to get those things out for me."

"About that. If you were going to tell the maid service to put them back out where they'd picked them up from, why did you have them put them away in the first place? I mean, I'm here. I would see them."

Myra gasped, "Unless they really do all go in here. In her bedroom!"

"Put the pictures back up where you found them and never mention this again, and I might continue allowing you to live in my home."

"I think I need to talk to Jag. I think you've come between us because you have feelings for him. And I think you don't want him with me."

"You know that I don't want him with you," she said with a ton of attitude. "You're getting a great deal here, Millie. Don't be a dumbass and blow it by being stupid."

"He isn't the kind of man who would take our baby away from me," I said, knowing I was right.

"How would you know what kind of man he is?" Samantha asked. "You've known him for less than twenty-four hours. You don't know him at all. You have no idea what he is or is not capable of doing. He and I do have more to our relationship than either of us has ever let on. We like to keep things just between us. But all that is about to come out, and I won't let you and that bastard you are carrying wreck my plans. As a matter of fact, your pregnancy has sped up my plans."

"Your plans?" I asked, thinking that Jag probably didn't have much, if anything, to do with these plans of hers.

"Jag is spoken for, Millie. That is all you need to know. He's not available to be anything to you or any other woman."

"What does that even mean?" Myra asked with confusion in her voice.

I knew what it meant. "It sounds to me like Samantha has designs for Jag that he probably isn't aware of."

"If he's not aware of them, then why are we in the same bed right now?"

The screen lit up—she had switched the call to a Facetime call. Swiftly, I accepted the call, and sure enough, there was Jag, sleeping in the bed that she lay on.

"Why does he have clothes on?" Myra asked. "And his shoes aren't even off."

I had a terrible feeling about what I was looking at. And when Samantha turned the camera to show me her wiggling fingers, I saw a huge diamond ring and wedding band on her finger. "He drank a bit too much when we celebrated our marriage. Jag's not a big drinker."

"Marriage?" I said, shock taking over. "He married you?"

"He most certainly did. And I'm not letting some little homewrecking tramp ruin our beautiful marriage. I assume you know that you can get the fuck out of our Miami home."

I should have known not to trust her.

"You will not get away with this."

She laughed and ended the call.

But the laugh was on her as I took the napkin with Jag's number out of my purse and made the call I should have made the day he left Shiner.

The call was answered, and I heard a noise that sounded as if the phone had fallen to the floor. "Shit," I heard Jag shout with a slurred voice. "My phone."

"Just be still," I heard Samantha say with a soft voice. "I'll get it for you."

"Miss Petty, what was in the drink?"

And then that was it. The call ended right there.

Myra shook her head. "A man does not call his wife Miss Petty. Am I right?"

"I would think that you're right. So, what the hell is going on?"

Changing tactics, I texted Jag, telling him that it was me and to call me as soon as he could. But I couldn't rely on Samantha not deleting the text.

"He asked about something in his drink," Myra said. "Do you think she drugged him?"

"I have no idea what that woman is capable of doing." My heart pounded and my mind was racing. What could I even do to help when I was so far away from Jag? And then something Samantha had said to me earlier clicked in my mind. "They're at Jag's home in Dallas."

"We can't get there any time soon," Myra said. "But taking the Corvette would be the fastest way."

"I'm not thinking about driving there." I looked up a number and called it. "But I can send someone to him."

"Dallas police department, how can I direct your call?" a woman answered.

"Hi. I need to see if anyone there can check up on a friend of mine who lives in Dallas. But I don't have his address," I let her know.

"Sounds like you want an officer to make a wellness check on your friend. If you know the name of the homeowner, we can find the address. Can you tell me why you feel the need to have him checked on?"

"His assistant and I were on a video call. My friend was passed out on the bed, wearing all of his clothes, including his shoes. When I called his cell phone, he dropped the phone, and I heard him asking his assistant what was in his drink. I'm very worried about him."

"Okay, and your name is?"

"Millie Powers."

"And his name is?"

"Jag Briggs."

"And who owns the home you think he's in?"

"Jag Briggs owns the home, from what I understand."

I heard her tapping on a keyboard, then she said, "We do have an address for him. I'll send an officer over right away."

"Can I be informed of the situation?" I asked, as worry had taken over.

"Is this a good number to reach you at?" she asked.

"Yes, it is."

"I will take it down and send it to the officer who takes this assignment. I'll make sure they know to give you a call once they know what's going on. Have a nice day."

As if my day was going to be nice at all. Trusting Samantha had been the biggest mistake I had ever made. And what was even scarier was the ride my sister and I were about to take. "Pack a bag, Myra, and make it small. We're going to Dallas, and we're taking the Corvette. I've got to get to Jag as fast as I can to tell him about our baby."

With a nod, Myra jumped into action. "We can switch out the driving and go straight through. I'll take the night shift. I love driving at night."

"Just don't kill us, please." I was on the verge of making things right for all of us. The last thing I wanted was to end up in a wreck the way our parents had.

I got to work packing a bag for myself. I was thankful that I had done what had come naturally to me by being so frugal. I hadn't spent a dime of the money Samantha had sent to me. I had more cash at my disposal than we would ever need to get to Jag.

Within the hour, Myra and I were pulling out of the garage when my cell rang. "Hello?" I said. I didn't recognize the incoming number.

"This is Officer Jones from the Dallas Police Department. I'm looking for Millie Powers."

My heart stopped, and I put my foot on the brake, remaining in the driveway instead of pulling onto the street. "This is her."

"Put it on speaker," Myra said.

I pushed the button so that she could hear what the officer had to say. "We did find Jag Briggs inside the home. He was clearly inebriated but could speak. He seemed confused as to why he was so out of it. The woman with him was a good bit older than him and tried taking over, telling us that they'd gotten married that day and her new husband had celebrated a bit too hard."

"So, they are married?" I thought I was going to throw up again and held my stomach.

"I don't think so. She had on a wedding set, but he didn't have a ring on. So, that was suspect. Plus, he shook his head when she said that. I took it upon myself to call in an ambulance to take a sample of his blood and urine to determine if there are any drugs in his system. You said that you're his friend, right?"

"I am his friend, yes."

"Do you know if he uses drugs?"

"I don't think that he does. But I do think that his assistant might have slipped something into whatever drink she's given him." Rage began to mingle with the worry I already had going on.

I'm going to kill that bitch!

"Am I getting this right?" he asked. "You think the woman with him, the one you keep saying is his assistant, might've given him something without him knowing about it?"

"I do think that, yes," I confirmed. "Her name is Samantha Petty."

"He calls her Miss Petty," he said.

"He does call her that. She has been his assistant for a long time. She's known him since he was a kid of about eleven. And she's one hell of a devious woman."

"I could tell that something was just not right there. She keeps trying to take over and get rid of me and the paramedics. She keeps saying that she's got everything under control and there is absolutely no reason anyone should be worried about anything."

"Kind of crazy of her to say when Jag is so obviously out of it. Don't you think?" I asked.

"You know, I've got a gut feeling about her, and when I get that, I am rarely wrong. I'm going to have the paramedics go ahead and take Mr. Briggs to the hospital. I'm also going to take Samantha Petty into custody under suspicion of tampering with the drinks that she served to your friend."

"I'm in Miami right now. But I'm on my way to Dallas. I should be there sometime tomorrow. If you could let him know that Millie is on the way to him and also text me what hospital he's in, that would be great."

"I will do that for you. Thank you for calling this in. Your call might have averted a tragedy here today."

"He means a lot to me. Thanks for calling to let me know what's going on."

Putting the phone down, I sighed with a little bit of relief. "Okay, so now all we have to do is get to Dallas and try our best not to get pulled over for speeding."

And then I get to tell Jag that he's going to be a father.

Chapter Twenty-Three

Jag

"I can't believe Miss Petty would do something like this," I said as I walked out of the hospital the following morning.

One of my lawyers walked along with me, shaking his head. "While she's in custody, we need to comb through everything she touched to see if she did anything else that's illegal."

My cell rang, and I looked at the number, which I didn't recognize. "I wonder if this is Millie? The officer told me it was her who called in the wellness check yesterday." I swiped the screen. "Hello?"

"Jag?" I heard her sweet voice ask.

"Millie?"

"Jag!"

"Millie!"

"Oh, my God. How are you feeling?"

"Great now. Where are you?"

"On my way to you in Dallas. We were in Miami. Your assistant had us taken there. We were staying at her house. It's a long story, but I'll tell you everything."

"I'm going to save this number, and I'll text you my address. Come straight to me, Millie. I've missed you so much. You have no idea how much I've thought about you. And I'm so sorry for anything that woman did to you. I am with one of my lawyers right now. My team of them will be at my home too. We're going to comb through everything to see what else we can find out about Samantha Petty. Your testimony of what she did to you and your sister will be needed."

"Okay. We're ready to tell them everything."

"It's good to hear your voice, Millie. It really is. I can't wait to see you."

"Me too, Jag. The GPS says we should arrive in Dallas in two hours. We drove straight through, trading off driving to get to you as fast as we could."

"Your sister is old enough to drive?"

"Yeah. She got her license this year. She's got in a lot of practice with this long drive."

"You two be careful," I cautioned them. "I don't want anything to happen to you. See you soon. Bye now." I already felt better just from talking to her. "I think most of this has to do with some weird jealousy thing my assistant had over the woman I just spoke to."

"Samantha did pretend you two were married. So, I would bet you're right about the jealousy being a catalyst for all she's pulled here lately." He and I got into his car and headed to my place.

When I saw Millie being brought into my office, all that worry and strife melted away as we ran to each other and held each other tight. "My God, it's good to see you, Millie."

"Jag, you have no idea how good it is to see you and how much I have to tell you."

Another girl, younger than Millie, waved at me as I looked at her over Millie's shoulder. "Hi, Jag. I'm Myra. Millie's younger sister."

I let Millie out of my arms, but I didn't want to let her go completely so I held firmly to her hand. "It's nice to finally meet you, Myra. Let's go sit down and talk about all this craziness."

Millie didn't move with me. Instead, she pulled my hand, tugging me to stop. "Jag, I need to tell you something in private before we do anything else."

Looking back at Myra, I saw she was nodding. "Go. I'll be fine here."

"Come on, we can go into the next room, Millie."

"Thanks, Jag." She walked with me to the next room, where I closed the door, giving us all the privacy we'd need.

I couldn't help myself and pulled her into my arms, placing a kiss on her warm lips. "You have no idea how much I've missed you."

Gazing into my eyes, her body melted into mine, and she whispered, "I've missed you too. And I've got something to tell you—something I pray you'll be happy about."

Moving backward with her, I didn't stop until the backs of my legs hit the sofa. Then I sat, pulling her with me to sit on my lap. "I'm sure I'll be happy with anything you say, Millie. I'm just about as happy as I've ever been in my entire life with you here now."

"Good. I'm happy too, Jag. Very happy. See, I had been just about to call you the day Samantha came to the diner to see me."

"You were going to call me that day?" I couldn't believe it. "So, what happened? Why didn't you call?"

"I made the mistake of telling your assistant something that I shouldn't have. And that's when she got to work, making sure you and I stayed far away from each other. She made me question things about you—about your character."

"She did?" I had the feeling that more and more things were going to come out that would leave me disillusioned with my former assistant. "For the record, she's fired. And we're looking for all we can find to put her in prison too. So, you have nothing to worry about where she's concerned. And neither do I."

"I'm glad to hear that. And I hope you're going to be glad about what you're about to hear." She licked her lips, looking as if she was trying to build up the courage to tell me something.

"Go for it, baby. There is nothing you can say that will make me any less happy than I am right now with you here."

Taking a deep breath, she said quietly, "Jag, you and I are having a baby. I'm twelve weeks as of yesterday."

I wasn't sure I'd heard her right. "You're what now? Twelve weeks? You and I are..."

"Having a baby," she finished for me. "We're going to be parents."

"And was this why you were going to call me that day? To tell me that you're pregnant?"

"Yes. I'd just taken the pregnancy test. I hadn't even realized that I was late until my sister brought something up. So, I left work without telling anyone a thing. I bought a pregnancy test, took it home, and it was positive. I was sort of in shock."

"And then what happened?"

"Well, I went back to work because we were swamped. I had already decided to call you as soon as things slowed down. But then Samantha showed up. And I was just not really thinking that anything bad could come of me telling her about the baby. I mean, I was going to call you right after she and I talked anyway."

"I know the shock you must've felt because I'm in shock right now. But I'm happy, Millie. I really am happy. And we're going to do everything together. I mean that."

Tears filled her eyes. "I was so stupid for listening to her. She put me through hell. She made me think that you were a bad man and would take our baby away from me."

"Never," I said, stroking her hair and kissing the top of her head. "I would never do anything to hurt you or our child. We're in this together, girl. Don't you doubt that for a moment."

"She said you would get your lawyers and take me to court and take the baby from me. And I was so scared. I didn't want to believe her, but I had to think about the baby and what was best for it. I kept telling her that I wanted to share it with you. But she just kept saying that I didn't know what you were like. That I'd only known the you that you let me see. She said you were selfish."

"Me?" I didn't have a selfish bone in my body. "Not me. Do you have any idea how much money I give to charity each year? A lot. A hell of a lot."

A knock came on the door, interrupting us. Millie looked at me, wiping her eyes with the backs of her hands. "You can see what they want. As long as I've told you the news, that's all I really care about. I just didn't want another second to go by with you not knowing about the baby."

Kissing her softly, I whispered, "I've never been happier in my entire life. Not ever."

And the news just kept getting better and better as we went out to learn that the lawyers had found proof that Miss Petty had been embezzling money from me for years. She would be spending a long time behind bars, and that made me even happier than I'd been before.

That night, Millie lay in my arms, in my bed, and the happiness I'd found rose even higher. "This is the best day ever."

Arching up to me, she moaned, "For me too."

"Just so you know, I think you've stolen my heart." Kissing a line up her neck, I nibbled her earlobe.

"Just so you know, I'm keeping it." Her nails dug into my back. "Oh yeah, right there, babe. So right that it can't be wrong."

Pulling my head back, I looked into her eyes. "And where might your heart be, my love?"

"You should know," she said with a sexy smile. "It's yours."

"I'm not giving yours back either." Tapping my chest, I said, "It's right here, and this is where it's going to stay."

"Jag?" she asked as we moved in unison. "I know this is probably way too soon to be thinking about this, but the living situation…"

"You're staying with me. You and Myra. My homes are now your homes. I mean that."

"We're not even married," she said with a grin. "We're not even dating. Not really."

"We are *together*. And we're going to stay together. Not just for the baby either. I want you. Not a day has gone by since I left Shiner that I haven't thought about you and wished you would call me."

She chewed on her lower lip before saying, "I thought about you too. But I was afraid that what your assistant said to me before you guys left was true."

"Oh, yeah. Rachel told me about all that."

"Rachel?" She looked puzzled. "When did you talk to her?"

"Yesterday, when I went to see if I could find you. Miss Petty had lied to me about things too. But I was done believing that you left town with some other guy or just to make sure I couldn't find you because you didn't want anything else to do with me."

"As if I would leave town to hide from you. I don't hide from guys I don't like. I tell them to fuck off."

"That's what I thought too. But, just like you, I believed her. Sort of. Not entirely. Never entirely."

"Me neither. I kept having hope that she was wrong or even lying about you. She kept saying that I didn't know you. But I felt like I did know you. I knew the man she didn't. And I was right about that too. So, I feel super smart today."

Kissing her cheek, I let her know what I thought about her. "You are super smart in my eyes. And you're going to get that chance you've been waiting for to do what's best for you. Whatever you want. And—just so you know—I'm not the type of person who thinks college is the answer to everything. You can think outside the box with me, baby."

"That will take some time, Jag. I've been thinking about my sister and what would be best for her for such a long time that I'm not sure how to switch modes."

"I'm going to help you. And I'll let your sister know that she can do whatever she wants as well. I'm going to be here for you two. Always and forever. I've got your backs, is what I'm saying."

"That's nice to hear." With a sigh, she ran her arms around my neck, pulling me to her. "I'm going to cherish you, you know."

"As I will cherish you." Looking into her eyes, I saw my entire future right there in them. "We are going to be a happy family. I can promise you that."

"And I believe you." Pulling me closer, she kissed me, making my heart explode and sending fireworks directly to my brain.

If anyone had told me that I'd want to spend my life with a woman I'd known for less than a day, I would've told them they were crazy. But that's what happened.

Millie and I made promises to each other that night—our first night as a real couple and soon-to-be parents. That night, we made love, we made memories, and we made the foundation of what would become a very happy and stable family.

And one and a half months later, we made it all very legal when we got married, back in Millie's hometown. Lights were strung up everywhere, and music was pulling our guests to get on their feet and join us on the dance floor where Millie and I had fallen in love with each other.

Of course, the diner catered the event, and the whole town had been invited. And once the festivities were over, I carried my wife across the main street, down the road that led to the RV park where our colossal RV waited for us to consummate our marriage.

When we got to the RV, I saw that someone had taped a note to the door. "If the RV is rockin', don't come a knockin'," I read out loud.

"Has to be one of my goofy friends," Millie said as she laughed. "Small town people never change."

"That's good to know. I don't want any of us to change. Not too much. Good people need to stay good people." Opening the door, I carried my bride—as tradition dictated—over the threshold.

But once inside, I didn't carry her straight to bed. Instead, I put her feet on the floor. She looked at me with one wrinkle crossing her forehead. "You're not taking me straight to the bedroom to ravage me? I must admit I'm pretty disappointed. I've been imagining hot married sex for a month."

"That's next. I want to show you the wedding present that I got you first. It wasn't easy to get it done within a month's time, but as they say, money can make miracles happen." I stepped up on the seat of the dining table, reaching for her hand. "Come on, baby. This is the best place to see it from."

"You went and bought me a star, didn't you?"

Pulling her up with me, we took the next step to get on top of the dining table. Then I opened the skylight so that we could look out of it. I lifted her a bit so she could get a good look at what I'd given her. "Do you see that?"

"Um, well, I'm not sure. I can't seem to see that many stars because there's suddenly a lot of light coming from something over this way. Like a huge house or something. Maybe a hotel. I didn't know they were going to build one here, but that's got to be it."

"Nope. That's not a hotel. That's your wedding present."

"You built me a mansion right here in Shiner?" she asked with tears filling her eyes.

"I built us a home right here in your hometown, baby. Because I want you to be happy above all else. I love you."

Throwing her arms around my neck, her tears were wet against my skin as she said the words I loved to hear. "I love you too, Jag."

And we always will.

Epilogue

Millie

One year later...

"Myra, did you get your sweet baby niece to take her nap already?" I asked, as I swept through the main entrance of the bed and breakfast that I ran in Shiner.

She held up the baby monitor she had in her hand. "Quin is sleeping like the baby she is, and you'll be happy to know that using the soft classical music I've been playing each time I've put her to sleep has begun having the effects I thought it would. Once she heard the music, her little eyes closed, and she rested her head on my shoulder. She was asleep within a few minutes. I told you it would work."

"You did tell me that." I was proud of Myra. She'd made a decision to study childhood development—specializing in newborns—and was an expert on the best practices for caring for them.

Quin was now seven months old and had given Myra lots of data to use for her studies. Plus, Myra ran the daycare center at the bed and breakfast, so our guests could have a safe place to leave their children while they went out on the town to shop or have a drink or two.

My husband couldn't have been prouder of what we'd become. At first, he wasn't super cool with the idea of turning the mansion he'd built for me in Shiner into a business. But I showed him how only the first floor would be used for the bed and breakfast and the childcare facility. The upper two stories were for our family and nothing else.

He was so happy with the way I'd done things that he asked me if I wanted to do the same thing with any of our other homes. So, the home in Los Angeles was my next venture.

I love being an entrepreneur.

"Honey, I'm home," Jag called as he came up the stairs to our main living area.

Meeting him at the top of the stairs, I held my arms open for him. He ran his around me, pulling me into his warm embrace. His lips planted a kiss on top of my head, as usual. "How was today's tour?"

Jag had begun bringing in buyers from other countries to take them on tours of the brewery instead of going to other countries to market the beer made in town. And it had worked wonders.

The Briggs empire continued to grow. Our family would continue to grow too. It hadn't been planned, but while breastfeeding our daughter I hadn't been able to take any oral contraceptives. That had left us with the old-fashioned methods, which weren't nearly as good at protecting from the possibility of another pregnancy.

So, I had some news for my husband. But first, I listened to how his day had gone. "The Irish are a fiery sort. Full of jokes, laughter, and plenty of consumption of the product. So, I too imbibed in the dark spirit more than I normally do."

"Ah, so you're on the toasted side this evening," I said with light laughter.

"Yes, I'm in need of food. Starchy foods and bread that can soak up some of this stuff making waves inside my stomach." We walked, hand in hand, to the sofa where he fell back, pulling me with him.

I landed on top of the man I had come to love with more of my heart than I even knew I possessed. "I'll put in your order to our chef, and soon you will be enjoying something not only delicious but alcohol-filtering as well. But first, you and I have something to celebrate."

He looked a little worried as he asked, "It's not our anniversary, is it?"

"Nope." Looking down at him, I had the thought that I loved looking at him in that position the best. "It's not something that you've forgotten."

"That's good. What is it then?" He hiccuped. "Excuse me."

I could smell the stout beer on his warm breath and wrinkled my nose before jumping off him and running to the nearest bathroom, where I promptly threw up.

When I turned around, I found him standing there, leaning his broad shoulder against the door frame. "Was my breath really that bad?"

"No," I laughed as I took the wet washcloth he handed me and wiped my face.

His smile told me more than his words did, as he asked, "Do you have a stomach bug?"

"No," I said as I got off my knees, no longer worshiping the porcelain god. I straightened my clothes, ran one hand through my hair, and took a cleansing breath. "I need to brush my teeth. I'll be right back."

He followed me as I went to our bedroom. "No stomach bug. My breath didn't gross you out that bad. So, what could've made you toss your cookies like that?"

"None of those things." I put a fair amount of toothpaste on my toothbrush, then tried to scrub the acidic taste of stomach acid from my mouth.

"Did you eat something questionable today? Should I call the doctor to come and pay you a visit?"

"No." Rinsing my mouth with water, I cleaned all the sudsy toothpaste out of it. Then I picked up the bottle of minty mouthwash and filled the little paper cup that I pulled from the dispenser next to the sink.

"Okay, so nothing bad on your stomach either. I'm not crazy about the fact that you're puking and have no reason for it. To be honest, it worries me."

With my breath all fresh again, I turned to him, draped my arms around his shoulders, and smiled, feeling a lot more confident with myself. "You like being a father, don't you?"

"I love it." His hands moved to hold me at the waist. "Do you like being a mother?"

"I also love being a mother. And since we both love being those things, I think that you'll be as happy as I am about the news that I'm about to give you."

The sound of someone screaming filled the air. "Ahhh! Yes! Yes!"

I had no idea why my sister would be shouting something like that as she ran through the house. "Myra?" I asked as my husband and I let go of each other.

We met her in our bedroom. Her smile was as wide as it could be, and she held up something I'd left in the trash can in the bathroom in the hall. "We're having another baby!"

Jag looked at me with cocked brows. "You and me? Or your sister and someone we've never met yet?"

Myra smacked her fist into Jag's strong arm. "You and my sister, you silly man. Congratulations! Quin will be the best big sister any child could ever have. And I will gain even more knowledge of newborns. It's a win-win, if you ask me."

Looking at my sister, I asked, "Do you think you can give me and my husband a moment to celebrate in private?"

"Oh!" she said as she backed out of the room. "Sorry. Did I steal your thunder, Millie? I honestly didn't mean to do that. I was just so excited and didn't think before I acted."

Jag gave me a little hug before he said, "There was no better way to learn of my next baby than his aunt shouting the news from the rooftops."

"His?" I asked Jag—I had no idea what our baby would turn out to be.

"Well, there's a fifty-fifty chance this one will be a boy, right?" he said, with that charming smile that melted my heart every single time.

"Yeah, there's a chance," I said. "So, you're happy about this, even though we didn't plan it?"

"Millie, we haven't planned anything that's happened so far. Why start trying to plan things now?"

Jag

Six months later...

The sting of a February winter snow took my breath as I ran into the hospital in New York. He'd come early. Two months earlier than the doctor had said he would. We were unprepared and unequipped for him—not that he seemed to care a bit.

"Can you believe he's got the lungs to scream like that?" the nurse asked the doctor who was in the middle of delivering our baby. "I thought you said he was premature. That doesn't sound premature to me."

I looked at Millie, who lay on the hospital bed. Her face was red, her breathing erratic, and she looked shocked. "He's okay, isn't he?"

"Sounds like he's got great lungs," I said to encourage her.

"One more push, Mrs. Briggs," the doctor said. "He'll be completely out then."

Millie looked at me with major wrinkles running along her forehead. "There's no more contractions. What does that mean?"

I looked at the nurse and doctor who stood at the other end of the bed. "Well, what does that mean?"

They didn't say a word. But the nurse walked across the room to get something from a drawer.

Millie wasn't going to just let it go. "What are you going to do?"

"Use forceps," the nurse said as she took out something silver and shiny that resembled the tongs we used to serve food at home.

"You are going to do what with those?" I asked.

"Pull your baby out," the doctor told me.

I watched as he used the tong-looking things the same way one did to remove a rack of ribs from a barbeque grill, moving in to retrieve my still-screaming son. "Um, no. You are not going to smash my son's head with those things."

"There's no other choice. He's not moving forward, and she doesn't seem able to push him out," the doctor said.

Giving my wife a look that said she was going to have to rally and do whatever she needed to do to get our son out of her body without the use of freaking barbeque tongs, I asked her one question. "Do you love me?"

Nodding, she said, "You know I do."

"Okay, so you are going to give this your all. I mean, you're gonna dig down deep."

Wearing a frantic expression, she said, "Jag, you don't understand. I'm not having any more contractions."

"I'm going to have to use the barbeque tongs," the doctor said, then shook his head. "I mean, the forceps. His chest is compressed."

Cocking my head to one side, I looked my wife straight in the eyes. "You can do this. It's a simple maneuver. Push. Bear down. I have seen you do it before. You can do it now. Our son needs you to do it. Push, baby. Push for all your worth. Set our son free!"

Looking into my eyes the whole time, she began taking deep breaths, then her eyes closed and she made a horrible sound. I could not believe what I heard or saw.

Her face—already red—turned purple as she growled like a demon. My skin pebbled with goosebumps, and the doctor and nurse stood there with mouths gaping.

"You got this, baby!" I shouted encouragement.

The baby's cries got quiet, then went away entirely. My wife's face went from purple to nearly black as she refused to give up her pushing.

I heard a sickly sound, and then the doctor shouted, "You did it!"

"You did it!" I cried out, then leaned over to kiss my wife on the forehead. I said it much more softly the second time. "You did it, baby."

She finally exhaled, eyes still closed, color coming back to something more normal. "Is he okay?" she whispered hoarsely.

The nurse who now held our very quiet, premature son, nodded at us as she took him to the waiting neonatal staff who'd been standing by, waiting to see if our boy would make it or not.

"He's going to be okay, little momma," I whispered in my wife's ear.

She whispered back, "There's some Elvis in you, and you know it." And then she opened her eyes.

I tried not to gasp, but the sound came out anyway.

"What?" she asked.

Her doctor came over to me, looking to see what I'd gasped about. "Oh! Well, that's completely natural."

I didn't want to scare Millie. "How long before they're back to normal?"

"Jag?" Millie asked, with concern etching her voice. "What's wrong?"

I looked at the doctor for answers. "So, all sorts of things can cause the blood vessels in the eye to burst."

"What?" Millie asked, looking as if she was about to cry.

I took her hand in mine. "Baby, it's going to be fine." I turned to the doctor for confirmation on that. "Right?"

He nodded. "Yes. Of course, it will all go back to normal. It's like a bruise. No bruise lasts that long. Two weeks or so. That's it. Most of the time."

"You've never heard of this lasting like, forever, right?" I had to ask.

"Damn it, Jag," Millie whimpered. "What's wrong with me?"

"Well, your eyes are like totally bloodshot. Like, completely red. There is no white in them—at all." Running my hand over her head, I let her know the one thing she needed to know. "Hey, it's gonna fade away. And even if for some strange reason it doesn't, guess what?"

Mouth in a horseshoe, she asked, "What?"

"I will still love you. You will still be my wife. You will still be the mother of my children. And life will go on."

"Can I have a mirror?" she asked.

The nurse came to Millie's side with not only a mirror but her cell phone out. "So, this is you now." She put the mirror in front of my wife's face. "And before you get upset—here's a picture of me one week after the same thing happened to me after I got totally drunk one night and had a hangover from hell where I threw up violently. See? It goes away faster than you think it will."

Millie looked back at me with one question on her rosy, red lips, "So, are we still going to have our happily ever after, Jag?"

With a kiss on the top of her head, I let her know how life was going to go for us, "We have found our happily ever after, and we will not let it go for anything."

The End

Other Books in This Series

Marriage by Mistake[1]
Cowboy Protector[2]
Fake it for Real[3]

---

1. https://www.amazon.com/gp/product/B0BB91MQJK
2. https://www.amazon.com/gp/product/B0BF77CQR2
3. https://www.amazon.com/gp/product/B0BH6TWGTR

CPSIA information can be obtained
at www.ICGtesting.com
Printed in the USA
LVHW081103210223
739961LV00004B/484